THE PATRON

BOOK ONE OF THE BROKEN SLIPPER TRILOGY

VIVIAN WOOD

AUTHOR'S COPYRIGHT

This book would not have been as special or nearly as well-loved without my beta team — Patricia and Amanda particularly! I would also like to thank Antje, Jeanette, and all my other eagle eyed early readers… you all are the bee's knees!

Want to hear a playlist of songs that inspired The Patron? Click here to see it on Spotify.

1. Bad Girls — M.I.A.
2. God is a woman — Ariana Grande
3. lovely — Billie Eilish, Khalid
4. Without Me — Halsey
5. Big Wave — Jenny and Johnny
6. Liberation — Outkast, Cee-Lo
7. Midnight City — M83
8. goodnight n go — Ariana Grande
9. Lowly Deserter — Glen Hansard
10. Grandloves — Purity Ring, Young Magic
11. Once In My Life — The Decemberists
12. Honey — Kehlani

13. The Book of Love — The Magnetic Fields
14. 6 Underground — Sneaker Pimps
15. Savage Remix — Megan Thee Stallion, Beyoncé
16. Roads — Portishead
17. Slide — H.E.R., YG
18. Angel — Massive Attack
19. I Need My Girl — The National
20. Two Weeks — FKA Twigs

Enjoy the book!

KAIA

"One, two, three, four," Melanie, our instructor counts off. She speaks in a high pitched, nasal voice. The piano music starts once again. "Girls! Group one, move forward. And one, two, three... *pir-ou-ette.* Now *pir-ou-ette...* good, good."

Her lilting Irish voice is set to the rhythm. As one, the group ahead of me neatly spins on their tiptoes, executing flawless pirouettes. The whole room is mirrored, floor to ceiling, with a sturdy wooden barre bolted to every inch. With the mirror, it looks like twenty four perfect ballerinas are finishing their pirouettes.

It makes sense, because this class is the best of the best. The most dedicated ballerinas and danseurs, the ones who have given up regular school and any semblance of their social lives to be here. After most would-be dancers are bounced from the program for not following the rules or just plain not being good enough, this is what you have left.

The *hardcore* dancers. I've worked my ass off to be in this final class.

I suck in a breath and stretch my neck, readying myself for my group.

Melanie claps along on a steady, brisk four count. "Next group! And one, two, three… *pir-ou-ette*. And *pir-ou-ette…*"

My arms swoop out to the sides as I lift onto my tiptoes and twirl. The motion is automatic, one born of muscle memory more than anything else. I'm directing most of my attention at my feet and the slight curve in my back. I usually get in trouble for my feet not pointing enough or my back not having a slight bow in it if I'm not intensely concentrated.

"Kaia! There should be more arch to your arms!" Melanie admonishes me. I give my arms a little more lift and she bows her head quickly. "There you go."

I don't have time to look around at the twelve other ballerinas in my group. I'm focused entirely on my feet and my back and the position of my arms. When I finish though, I realize that I've stopped very close to Manon, a little brunette ballerina who shoots me a glare.

I'm quick to move away, straightening my spine. Out of every ballerina in this school, Manon is by far the most caustic. And usually, her barbs are aimed at me.

"Sylvie! Don't start like that, how can you expect to be graceful if you start in such an ugly position?" Melanie calls, her expression stern. She tucks a strand of her dishwater blonde hair behind her ear, rolling her eyes. "Boys! Group one, forward please… And one, two, three… *pir-ou-ette*. And *pir-ou-ette…* Mason, that was perfect."

I glance to my right, catching myself in the mirror. A thin blonde ballerina stares back at me, wearing a lilac leotard, a filmy white dancer's skirt, opaque white tights, and ballet pink pointe shoes. I bite my lip and send my image a tiny frown; I immediately see the glaring flaws in my own appearance.

My father's voice echoes through my head.

Your hair is the wrong shade of blonde. Your nose is too big, your eyes are too far apart. You're too tall to do ballet, too heavy for most dancers to lift. Your posture is imperfect. Your feet are too large.

I swallow and lift my chin. I have to overcome my obvious shortfalls, be resilient enough to make it as a dancer. My dad put me through ballet academy and he has certain expectations.

If I work hard, if I focus all my energy on each and every move, I should be able to prevail.

But by far the worst thing of all is that I lack mobility in my turnout. The rotation of my hip joints, to turn outward away from the front of my body, is sadly never going to be a perfect one hundred and eighty degrees.

I wrinkle my nose at myself and drag my eyes back up to the rest of the class. I see my group moving forward again and I rush to take my place. We execute another set of pirouettes under Melanie's eagle-eyed gaze.

"Ella, you are still a step behind everyone else. Always a step behind. Start earlier."

The incredibly tiny black woman blushes and bows her head, but says nothing. I would kill for Ella's diminutive height or turnout, but I am incredibly glad not to get that same bit of criticism from our teacher.

"Let's change it up," Melanie says. She turns around, signaling to the piano player to stop. "This will be the last combination. Girls, please begin with relevé developé, pas de bourre, arabesque en diagonal, tombé, and demi-plie. Okay? Let's go."

The hardest part of my day is right now, when we've already had an full day of classes and we only have a few minutes more. The last fifteen minutes always seem to drag terribly.

We go through the combination two more times, with Melanie correcting everything she sees. Don't get me wrong, I know that she's one of our most kind hearted teachers. But by the time the class ends, I'm done with her critiques.

Honestly, I could probably use a day off right about now. But between attending my last month of classes here at the New York Academy of Ballet and my much less prestigious night job, there's a snowball's chance in hell of that randomly happening.

I walk over to grab my bottle of water, taking a long pull. As I'm guzzling down the water, Eric walks up. I gulp as he casually starts talking to me; with his blonde hair, clear blue eyes, and his muscular danseur's frame, Eric looks like a freaking Disney prince.

"Hey," he says, picking up a small black duffel bag from against the wall. "That last round of combinations was killer. I feel like I just got my ass kicked."

Before I even say a word, my face grows hot. As a ballerina, I'm always sensitive to my body and the story told by my posture. But talking to gorgeous Eric brings a whole new level of embarrassment and self consciousness.

I give him a shy smile. "Yeah, especially the last one. That releve développe sliding into that pas de bourrée was really tricky."

Eric nods, digging through his duffel bag. "I think that move is featured pretty heavily in The Nutcracker. So if we have any hope of getting picked for any ballet company, I guess that's a move we really have to nail." He pulls his water bottle out of his bag and takes a swig.

As he drinks, I look at the way his head is thrown back. His throat arches, his whole body effortlessly shifting to balance. I watch the motion of Eric swallowing, my eyes tracing the path of the water moving down his throat.

Will he ever ask me out? I wonder.

I've never been on a date or had a boyfriend, but I have definitely had the hots for Eric for years.

He snaps the lid closed on his water bottle and catches my longing expression. He arches an eyebrow. "What?"

My face goes red and I turn away from him, heading toward my own duffel bag. I fib a little. "Did you know that I can get extra life out of my pointe shoes by using floor wax? I dab a little inside the box, put the shoes in a preheated oven that's been turned off. When I take them out and let them cool overnight, they feel better and last longer."

He squints at me. "You are really thrifty, Kaia."

I am. I have to be.

There is no magical force out there, guiding me toward making money. Just me, trying to scrimp and save and cut corners to get by.

I flush, looking down at my hands.

Eric continues on, as if I had never started off on a

weird money saving tangent. "I'm just wondering about what company I'll end up in. Imagine if we both got accepted to the New York Ballet."

Manon is standing by the wall where my bag is. As I approach, she turns around, her lip curling into a delicate sneer.

"There is no way that Kaia will be chosen by the NYB. They only recruit five graduates from every ballet academy in the world each year. You just..." Her eyes scan my body, a smirk appearing on her lips. "Don't measure up. You should apply for Cincinnati or Birmingham or somewhere that they need second rate ballerinas, honestly."

My heart drops toward my feet. I open my mouth to return her snarky comment, but Ella walks over, inserting herself in the situation. Ella refuses to let anybody talk to her or her friends with disrespect... and I'm lucky enough that she has adopted me as one of her besties.

Whatever that means for ballerinas, anyway.

"Shut the fuck up, Manon. Don't you have a broomstick somewhere to polish up before the next full moon?" she says, making shooing motions with her hands. Her Southern accent is thick as molasses and twice as syrupy-sweet.

Manon's lips twist. "Go back to whatever hillbilly town you're from. Leave the rest of the world alone."

"First of all, I'm from Marietta, which is a suburb of Atlanta. And second, you'd better watch your mouth before I clean it out with a fucking bar of soap." Ella says.

"Ugh, bitch." Manon storms off, disappearing through the studio door. I look at Ella, beyond grateful.

"Thanks," I say, shaking my head. "You always have the best retorts. I wish I was more like that."

Ella squeezes my upper arm. "Everybody does, boo."

She slides her gaze to Eric, her gaze tightening just a little. She doesn't completely approve of Eric for some reason and makes that pretty clear.

"Don't you have somewhere else to be?" she asks.

Eric gives her an odd look. "It's late Saturday afternoon. We're done with practice for the day. Where is it exactly that you think I should go?"

Ella puts her hand on her hip and rolls her eyes. She turns her attention back to me. "I'm going to see a play tonight. Any interest in attending?"

I wrinkle my nose and pull off my point shoes. "I can't. I have to work. Raincheck?"

"Sure," she says with a shrug.

Ella pulls a pair of dark sweatpants out of her duffel bag, quickly swapping her white skirt for the pants. I unwrap my laces and pull off my shoes. Eric is pulling on a pair of pants and a tight ivory sweater.

For a minute, the studio is quiet, the sound of everyone changing and moving out of the room dominating the space.

Ella pulls her pink fleece jacket on over her white leotard and then pulls her duffel bag strap onto her shoulder. I zip my jeans, shove my feet into my pink Converse, and pull a dark oversized fleece jacket on my body.

As soon as I shoulder my bag, Ella starts gently ushering me towards the door. "Hey, speaking of the auditions for the New York Ballet. Did you guys get a casting call in the mail?"

Eric nods, following us. "Yeah. The audition dates for people from our academy are the first through the fourth of next month."

My hands tighten on the strap of my duffel bag. I look down the long hallway lined with rehearsal rooms and instructor's offices, toward the white metal door at the very end. "I can't believe that we are less than a month away from auditions," I confess.

Eric snorts. "I auditioned for San Francisco last week. We are firmly within audition season, I think."

"I did Atlanta two weeks ago," Ella adds. "It was nice to get to see my folks. I didn't want them to realize that I will choose Atlanta as a last resort, though. I've got my eyes on someplace here in New York."

"Yeah, I really want to stay here," I say, nodding. "I'm actually only applying to a few places."

Eric shakes his head and hikes his duffel bag up on his arm. "I applied to ten companies. I want options."

I reach the doorway at the end of the hall first. Shouldering it open, I shiver against the cool New York City fall. As I hold the door for Ella and Eric, I glance at the soon to be setting sun where it peeks out from a gap between two towering skyscrapers.

The three of us walk toward the busy sidewalk. At this hour, the streets of Manhattan are packed with people of every description. Every color, every gender, every sexual orientation. It makes me breathe a little easier.

In New York City, I have a lot more anonymity and autonomy than I could ever have found if I'd just stayed in buttoned up, privileged Hartford. That's where my family is from and probably one of my least favorite places on the planet.

I heave a sigh as we all begin to head our separate ways.

"I'll catch you guys later," I say, shooting Eric and Ella both a little smile.

"Have fun working at the laundromat," Eric says, lifting a hand in a wave.

My cheeks stain red again. I definitely don't work at a laundromat. That's just the first thing that came to mind when Eric first asked me about my job. "Thanks," I manage.

"Bye," Ella says, already moving away.

I turn and start walking quickly toward the closest subway station. Pulling my cell phone out to check the time, I see that I've missed three calls from home. Sucking in a deep breath, I realize that I don't have time to call my father back. That causes a ripple of unease to slide down my spine.

My father doesn't have the best temperament when I am at his beck and call; when I miss his phone calls, he morphs into a sinister, dark character with a serious anger problem.

But I absolutely cannot be late for work. I need this job too much to screw around and get fired. Maybe if I am very lucky, I'll be able to call my dad back while I make the quick trip from the station to the club…

Chewing on my lower lip, I shove my phone into my duffel bag and hurry down the steps to the subway.

2

CALUM

I throw open the door to my penthouse loft, peering down at a young brunette. In her black pencil skirt, white button up blouse, and black peacoat, she's dressed for the office. Her dark hair is pinned up in a messy bun and she clutches several binders and file folders to her chest.

"Hi," she says, smiling a little breathlessly. "Mr. Fordham?"

I lean out of the doorway, glancing around at the neat white waiting room. If I was hoping for some sign of who this girl is, I'm disappointed. There is no one else with her except the closing doors of the elevator.

"How did you get up here?" I ask.

Her cheeks color. "I asked the man at the front desk to allow me to bring you some things from work."

I stare at her, trying to puzzle out what exactly she means. I feel caught off guard and a little bit underdressed; I make it a rule to wear a full three piece suit everywhere but here at my home and at dance rehearsal.

When I don't answer right away, she blushes and tucks her hair behind her ear. "Maybe you don't recognize me. I'm Amy? I work as a personal assistant at Indica Tech corporate. I'm one of your PAs."

I breathe out through my nose, my lips twisting. "Is there a reason you are bothering me at my home, Amy?"

She sucks in a breath. "I brought you the sales reports. They took longer than I thought, so you'd already left the office by the time they were done. And I know that they carry sensitive information, so…" She flashes a timid smile. "Here I am."

I arch a brow. Amy's story is bullshit. There were at least four people that I already know that she could have given a report to. So her being here is for some other reason.

Eying her up and down, I heave a sigh. Backing up, I wave her into the foyer of my apartment. "Come in."

She tucks her hair behind her ear again and gives me a wide-eyed look. It's tinged with a little longing.

Ah. That's why she's here. Why she broke several rules at work just to be strolling in my front door right now.

I smirk a little. Amy wants to catch my eye. She wants me to kiss her, to seduce her. Hell, she probably wants a big fucking ring on top of all that.

It's what women seem to want from me ever since my business went public at a hundred dollars a share.

I don't bother to close the front door. Instead, I stick out a hand and cock my head. "Well?"

Amy swallows, her eyes darting toward the sleek, dark

furnishings of the next room. She fumbles around, producing a sheaf of papers.

I snatch them from her hand, giving the top sheet a cursory examination. Amy rocks on her feet a little nervously, glancing again at the living room.

"Do you mind if I just put my things down so I can fix my heel?" she asks.

I narrow my eyes on her face, folding the sheaf of paper in half. "If you must."

She hurries into my expansive, elegant living room with some awe. Everything in this room looks expensive because it is; made of teakwood and dark leather, the furniture in here practically shouts *I'm wealthy*.

Amy collapses on a couch as I follow her into the room. I cross my arms and shoot her a little glare. She pushes the binders a little ways away from her on the couch, pulling one of her shoes off.

She looks up at me as she massages her foot. "Thanks for letting me sit, Mr. Fordham. Or do you prefer Calum?"

I squint at her. "Whatever gets you the fuck out of here the fastest."

She blushes. "You're too much, Calum! I can't believe I'm in your house. If you'd asked me this morning, I'd have told you that you were crazy."

Her words strike the wrong note for me. Either she's smart and she's been planning this for a long time… or she's dumb and just an opportunist.

She's either dishonest or sloppy. Neither of which I find particularly appealing in the women I sleep with.

Just like that, the decision is made. I'm not going to entertain this woman tonight.

I whip out my phone, sending a text to my brother, who is already on his way here anyway. Then I give Amy a cold little smile.

"You're either a liar or a slob," I say, enunciating every word. "Either way, you fucked things up. Bringing this report here without checking in with your supervisors was extremely risky, Amy."

"Oh, I didn't mean to say—"

I cut her off with a sharp shake of my head. "I don't know what you were hoping to get out of coming to my house and invading my space. Maybe you just wanted to see the inside of your billionaire boss's home. Maybe your motivations are more nefarious." I shrug my shoulders. "Either way, I think it's safe to say you made an error."

Her chin wobbles. Her big brown eyes are wide and brimming with tears.

Seeing her reaction just makes me angrier. I pace around her in circles, shoving a hand through my dark undercut hair.

"Mr. Fordham, if you will just let me explain," she says. Her voice sounds breathy; any moment now, she will burst into tears.

It makes me hate her. Her presumptive, weakness, her assumption that I couldn't resist her because I'm a red blooded male… it turns my stomach. Tonight Amy finally lit the touch paper by bringing me reports that rightfully should've been given to me hours ago.

This is why I usually only sleep with high class escorts. I dictate the terms, they accept them. It's all a transaction to them and I'm left with zero guilt or remorse.

"Do you think I got to be the CEO of Indica Tech from filing reports late?" I bite off.

She draws a breath, shaking her head. "No, sir."

I crumple up the report in my hands, disgusted. "No. I didn't get all this," I wave my hands to indicate our surroundings. "This penthouse in downtown Manhattan, the offices in Midtown, my fleet of cars and private planes, Indica Tech, and Indica Charities. None of it was earned through the kind of sloppy work that you have been showing recently."

Her throat works. Tears brim in her eyes, spilling over on one side. She gives her head a sharp shake. "I understand."

I cock my head, staring at her. "Do you?" I look her up and down. "If you want to keep working here, you'll do better. Turn things in on time. Dress appropriately for work. And under no circumstances should you ever just drop by your boss's home with such a flimsy excuse."

Her eyes widen. "Are you going to fire me?"

I roll my eyes, shaking my head. "No. I don't fire people. I'm too important to have to deal with that."

Right on cue, my brother Lucas appears in the doorway of the living room. Tall, broad, dark haired, and wearing a navy three piece suit, he could be my twin.

"Firing people is my job," he says, smiling thinly. He beckons to her. "Come along, Miss Blankenship. We should talk."

That's when she starts crying. She turns to me as if I'm about to save her. I think that this is perhaps the first time she has ever been rejected so soundly; first sexually, and now she's about to lose her job.

I make a shooing motion with my hand. "Get the fuck out."

She leaves my living room in a hurry, running past Lucas. He heaves a sigh, pushes off the doorframe, and trails after her.

I pace to the window, staring out at the dazzling view of downtown New York City. The sun has just sunk below the horizon and now the lights on the surrounding buildings are starting to come on.

I take a deep breath, willing my body to stop shaking. When I get angry, which is about once an hour, the emotion washes through me like a blood red wave. When I get furious, like I am right now, it's a struggle not to let the anger swallow me whole.

Anger has driven me far through life, all the way from our dingy childhood apartment to the most expensive penthouse in New York. It's what pushed me to be the best when I was a dancer; it put a chip on my shoulder that was so big, it brought the dance world to kneel at my feet.

I glance at my platinum wristwatch, grinding my teeth. Seven o'clock. A little early to be drinking, yes. But today was exceptionally trying. Turning to my bar cart, I uncork the Scotch and pour myself a couple of fingers.

"Go ahead and make me one too."

I glance back at my brother, my gaze narrowing. "That was fast."

He shrugs a single shoulder. "She was ready to get out the door."

I snort derisively. "I bet."

My hands have stopped shaking as I pour the second

drink. My brother, for all his faults, often provides the needed distraction at times like this.

I hand him the glass of scotch and walk to the other side of the room, sinking into my favorite chair. "I can't believe that she just showed up here, expecting…" I trail off for a second. "I don't actually know what she expected, honestly."

Lucas loosens his tie as he sits down on a black velvet and teakwood chair. "She expected to become Mrs. Fordham, I think. She said that she thought you liked her."

I wave a hand. "I'm done talking about her. Tell me what you found out today."

His expression hardens. "You should really be in the meetings with Omni, Calum. The CEO Jack Schwartz asked where you were and when he would meet you."

I push my cheek out with my tongue. "I'm trying to acquire his business and make him a rich bastard. He should be grateful, not asking questions."

"Well, he's still asking. Apparently he is quite religious and he's very concerned about selling to a degenerate. He actually gave me a whole lecture about how most billionaires get their money from unscrupulous sources and spend it on ungodly things. He really seemed focused on that."

"I fail to see how that has anything to do with me."

"Well, he asked why you aren't married. He said that he's skeptical that you two share the same vision, being that you haven't ever married." He scrunches up one side of his face. "I got the distinct impression that he was trying to make sure that you aren't gay."

I let out a surprised half laugh. "So what if I was?"

My brother steeples his fingers. "I think it would be a no-go."

"That's disgusting. If he didn't invent this new type of block chain cryptocurrency, I would tell him to fuck off." I lean forward, jabbing a finger into the dark wood of the coffee table. "I want that company, Lucas."

He holds up a hand. "I would argue that you need his company to develop IndicaTech any further."

I glare at him. "I don't need *anyone* outside of this room, Lucas."

He rolls his eyes. "Well, I have a bit of good news. It turns out that you and Jack have something in common." His lips curve upward. "His young daughter is heavily involved with ballet. He supports the New York Ballet, among other companies. From what I've found out, he is second only to you in terms of his patronage to their cause."

That gives me pause. I came from the world of ballet, back before I was a businessman. "That's… interesting," I allow.

"That's a way in," he says. "Use your mutual love of the ballet to your advantage."

I suck in a breath, thinking. "It would put me closer to Honor."

"I saw that the New York Ballet is going to do Sleeping Beauty in the spring. Maybe they need some sort of hands-on help."

I purse my lips. "Honor doesn't like that ballet, the last time I checked. She had her heart set on playing Giselle in the spring."

He rolls his eyes at me. "Honor this, Honor that. Look,

the prima at the New York Ballet has never even looked your way, brother. Just because you are the primary source is financial support for the ballet doesn't mean Honor is going to sleep with you."

"I'm not expecting her to," I growl.

Lucas purses his lips and gives me a droll look. "It's obvious enough that you are expecting that, Calum. You should forget her. As I've said before, you should be focusing on someone else." He draws in a breath, shaking his head. "Anyone else. One of the long list of ladies that you are plowing your way through."

My expression tightens a fraction. "I'm only twenty nine, Lucas. How many other men do you know that have risen from nothing to cradle the world in the palm of their hand?"

He sips the scotch, rising to his feet. "That's not really the point, is it?"

"That's exactly the point." I scowl at him. "Where are you off to?"

He places his glass on the bar cart, cracking his knuck-les. He hesitates for the slightest moment before folding his arms across his chest. "I'm on my way to drop some necessities off for Anita. Her nursing home called me and asked for a list of things."

At the sound of her name, my fist clenches around the glass tumbler. I struggle to keep my expression smooth and untroubled, but inside my guts roil.

"We have plenty of people to run those kinds of errands," I say evenly. "Send one of them."

Lucas rolls his eyes. "It's fine. I want to check in on her."

I narrow my eyes. "We don't owe her a damn thing, Lucas. Trust me," I grit out.

He turns toward the door, shaking his head. "After mom died, Anita took us in and raised us. She gave us warmth and security out of the goodness of her own heart. It doesn't seem like something that we should take for granted, no matter how far we've risen in the world since."

I know that he is ignorant of Anita's… needs. He's two years younger than me and I have done my best to keep him in the dark.

But damn if his words don't rankle me.

I glare at his back as he leaves. "Anita didn't do a fucking thing that didn't benefit her in some way. Just because you only see the ocean's surface does not mean that the sharks have all stopped circling."

He gives me half a wave as he leaves, leaving me alone with my bitter thoughts.

For a second, I think I can smell the heavy floral scent that Anita used to wear. Closing my eyes briefly, I see her reaching for me, a dangerous glint in her eyes. I clench every muscle in my body against her touch. In my mind's eye, she lets down her waterfall of dark, heavy hair. Her deep voice wafts over me. She pulls my hand up to rest on her breast, never dropping my gaze.

Don't you want to thank me, Calum?

I shake my head to clear that image, opening my eyes. My stomach lurches. I shoot to my feet, throwing back the last of my Scotch.

Suddenly, I feel the burning need to go to Club X.

3

KAIA

I frown down at my cell phone as another missed call goes to voicemail. I've now missed seven phone calls from my dad. Taking a deep breath, I turn the phone off completely and slip it into my locker.

My dad is probably leaving me another hate filled voicemail as we speak. If he knew where I am right now, knew what I was about to do to earn money, he would scream so loudly that I'm pretty sure he would have an aneurysm.

But I have to earn money. Enough money to pay my father back for every last cent he's ever spent on teaching me to become a perfect, graceful ballerina. I've calculated the cost and it is well over two hundred thousand dollars.

He's made it very clear that unless I come up with the money, I will follow his rules and do whatever he says until the day I die.

That knowledge slithers through my stomach as I close my locker and spin the combination.

"Lily, Brandie, Misty!" A dark-suited man sits by the door, reading off names. "One minute warning, girls."

Behind me, the dancers' changing room is loud and busy. Huge makeup mirrors and well-lighted white desks line one wall. White director's chairs are placed at intervals, each one of them currently supporting a stripper. They talk to each other as they lean close to the mirrors and perfect their lip gloss or apply another layer of blush.

I slide into the seat at the very end, feeling self conscious. I'm wearing what amounts to a tiny black bikini underneath a white kimono with clear six inch stilettos. My hair is teased and blown out, my makeup looks almost garish under the room's soft lights.

For any other job, I would look insane. Sliding a glance down the row of dancers, I feel like I fit in just fine.

"Candi, Baby, Daisy," the man sitting next door the door reads off. "You're up next, ladies."

The dancer to my left gets up just as Mia struts in the room. She sees me and comes over, her caramel-colored body glistening with baby oil and glitter. She clutches the top to her red bikini in one hand, tossing it on the desk as she throws herself into the chair beside me.

"Fucking cheap assholes," she says, sounding perky even though she's complaining.

She produces a neat wad of cash from the red triangle of fabric between her legs, shaking her head. She starts counting the cash as she glances at me. "I got a bunch of frat boys. They've obviously never been to a spot this nice and they didn't behave themselves. And to top it all off? They hardly tipped anything, even when I took them back to the private rooms. It was basically a huge waste of my time."

I scrunch up my face. "I hope you told security to kick them out."

She chuckles. "You're damn right I did."

I glance at her outfit, noticing a snag in her fishnets. I perk up. "You can fix that," I say, pointing it out to her. "A little hairspray and some clear nail polish will do the trick."

Mia flashes me a puzzled glance. "Girl, I do not have time to be fixing a pair of tights. The men like to rip them, I throw them away and buy new ones. It's the circle of life."

A tall, dark skinned dancer in a black babydoll dress stands up. "Anybody got some baby wipes? I ran out."

Mia glances over at her, then looks back at me, rolling her eyes. She leans closer to me. "No way am I giving that bitch anything. We double teamed a bachelor party together last week and I think she stole from me."

My eyes widen. "Really?"

Mia nods, wrinkling her nose. "Yep. I have no time or energy for these hoes. I'm busy working it, trying to find a patron."

I pause. "A patron?"

She looks at me with a sigh. "Yes. A patron. Someone that will pay for my services. Someone with a fat wallet that will take me out of here."

I bite my lip. "Pay for you to strip privately, you mean?"

She huffs out a laugh. "No, honey. Any man can get that here for a few hundred dollars. A patron gets you any way he wants it, as often as he feels like it. In exchange, he pays for an apartment, a car service, all the fancy clothes you could want…" She looks at herself in the mirror, leaning close to examine her reflection. "I've heard that a few girls even married their patrons."

My eyes widen. "Oh! That's pretty huge. I wonder what those girls did to get noticed?"

She shrugs, eyeing a group of girls coming through the door. I turn and look at them, laughing and wearing street clothes.

"New girls," Mia says, smacking her lips. "They all just turned eighteen, I bet. And they're wearing designer labels. If I had to put money on it, I would guess that they live at home with their rich daddies, who don't know that their little girls come here to get their ho on at night."

I purse my lips. "I bet you said something similar about me not that long ago."

"True. You have proven yourself, though. If your daddy has money, you wouldn't know it from looking at you." She pauses. "No offense. I'm just saying you don't act entitled."

I blow out a breath. "I am actually working here, trying to earn money to pay my dad back for private school. I'm never, ever going to owe anything to anyone ever again after working here for a year."

She arches a brow. "Owing your dad sounds like some white nonsense. You should be saving every penny and looking for ways to get to the next level."

"And what's that?"

"I already told you, girl. A *patron*." Her gaze catches on my white kimono. "I wouldn't wear that out on stage.

It's too light colored. It'll give you little fuzzy white balls in your armpits."

I glance down at my kimono, biting my lower lip. "I'm not planning on wearing it out there. It's just for comfort in here." Smiling, I stand up and head back to my locker. I swap the white kimono out for a black version, figuring it's better safe than sorry. "I am thinking of doing something a little different with my first routine, though."

Mia leans forward, snagging her top and putting it on. "More fancy ballet shit?"

My face goes hot red. "Yeah. You think it's a bad idea? I'm still on my month of probation with Club X…"

She looks at her teeth in the mirror, checking for lipstick. "I think you made a shit ton of money when you did that standing on your toes bit last week. Anybody would be crazy to tell you not to do it."

She eases out of her chair, her long legs gleaming as she stalks over to the lockers. I follow her, shrugging out of my kimono. As I put the robe away in my lockers, I whisper to Mia. "Hey, remember how I told you that I'm a dancer during the day too?"

She's changing into a different bikini, this one black pleather. "Uh… yeah, I guess I remember."

I scrunch up my face. "No one at my day job knows about this place. And vice versa. It's like… very much not allowed for ballerinas to…" I suck in a breath. "You know, dance for guys."

She closes her locker, favoring me with a smile. "Your secret is very much safe with me, honey."

"Cerise, Fawn, Latisha," the bored employee announces. "One minute till showtime."

Cerise. That's me. I take a deep breath, looking toward the doorway.

"See you a little later," I tell Mia. She smiles at me, counting her money again.

I totter toward the doorway, trying to make myself into Cerise. I start with my walk. Head held high, shoulders pulled back, arms nice and loose, lengthen my strides.

When I'm playing Cerise, I'm confident. Smiling. Teasing. Winking.

She likes men to look at her, to fawn over her tits and ass, to rain singles down as she slithers on the pole. She's my opposite in so many ways. I've never dated anyone, much less had strange men touch me as boldly as my customers will tonight.

Cerise is confident and worldly, I am introverted and naive. It's just easier to be Cerise for a while, a mask that I can slip off and leave in my locker at the end of the night.

Heading down the dark little hallway to the stage, I mount the steps and wait for the emcee to announce me. My heart rate rises. My smile stays plastered in place. In the seconds before I go onstage, it feels the same as it does when I'm waiting in the wings in my tutu and pointe shoes.

"Now appearing on the main stage, it's Cerise!"

My heart beat sounds like a drum in my ears. My music comes on, MIA's "Bad Girls". At the sound of the first notes, a switch is flipped for me.

There is a spotlight illuminating a shiny stripper pole on Club main stage. Everything around it is dim, made more so by my singleminded focus. I strut out onto the darkened stage, barely seeing the audience. All I can see is the stage, bare, waiting for me.

A shiver of excitement slides up my spine. I reach out for the pole, caressing it with one hand as I turn to face the audience. I don't really see them, though. Just the bright stage lights down front.

I grin and skim my fingers down my hip, biting my lip. Turning toward the pole, I slip my shoes off. As soon as I grip the pole and push onto my toes, a few whistles leave the crowd. I go into point briefly and the face away from the audience, leaning against the plot as I slide down into splits. I raise my arms over my head and then swing my hip around, grinding the ground beneath me. I keep a look of pleasure on my face as I get up, quickly turning it into climbing the pole and artfully sliding down. I step away from the pole and arch my back.

Taking a deep breath, I move away and focus on the audience members. A cluster of men in the front row grab my attention by waving a hundred dollar bill. I slide over to them, a knowing smirk on my face, and get on my knees. Plucking the bill from the customer, I push my breasts together and squeeze them. At the same time I spread my knees farther apart and run my hand down to the band of my bikini. Feeling naughty, I make sure to cup my pussy and pluck at my nipple, all the while making eye contact with the stage man.

Then I get on my stomach, never breaking eye contact, and slowly roll my ass so that I hump the floor in slow motion.

I don't see his reaction. I have no idea if it's good or

not. I'm just sucked into the performative nature of that slow body roll.

When I finally get up, I spread my legs wide and skim my bottoms down my legs. Bending over, I make sure that the customer gets the first look at my pussy.

Then I stride back to the pole. I lean my ass on the pole facing the audience, sliding down, an orgasmic expression on my face. Dollar bills rain down from above as I complete my splits, reaching above me to help myself back up. This time I go on my tiptoes with one foot, lifting the other high above my head. I lower my leg to the floor and raise my torso, steadying myself as my arms come up in an arch above my head.

I tear off my top, my breasts bouncing free. I climb the pole again and wrap my legs around it, dropping the piece of fabric and letting my entire body fall backward oh so slowly.

I let myself slide down until my hands can touch the floor. Then I gracefully round into a back bend and rise once more. Composing myself for a moment, I lift onto my tiptoes and execute a half-pirouette. Planting my right foot, I sweep my left leg skyward, then fold my body into the splits again.

All of this takes just a heart beat... or so it seems. Before I know it, the song shifts. The applause makes me turn pink.

I blink a few times and then run down to the end of the stage, collecting the cascade of dollar bills that I earned. After I sweep up most of them and grab my bikini, I hurry off stage. A minute later, I have my bikini on again and the money stashed in a little locked drop box beside the stage.

I didn't really have time to count, but the dollar bills felt weighty against my palm. One more step closer to independence.

I strut out to see at least five tables signaling to me that they want a private dance.

That's the least favorite part of my night. But at least guys are interested in what I can provide… I credit Mia with giving me tip to improve my onstage presence.

Lifting my chin, I'm about to walk toward the closest table when one of the dark-suited managers raises his hand to me.

I shoot him an odd look, but he continues waving me over. I look at the table of customers, hold up a single finger, and then scoot over to the bar.

He sniffs, rubbing his nose. "You got a guy waiting for you in the platinum room, darlin. The customer isn't a regular but he's very rich and very private. This customer is to be treated with kid gloves, you got it? Whatever he wants, you give." He looks me up and down. "Whatever's legal, anyway."

I am absolutely sure that he means all but the last part. My heart rate picks up. I nod my head, glancing at the tables.

"Hey," the manager says, snapping his fingers in front of my face. "Don't worry about them. Worry about the guy in the platinum room. You could easily make three or four times as much tonight as you would've normally. Now get going."

Eyes widening, I nod and scurry toward the Club's staircase. I bite my lip, trying not to look worried. Usually I'm not called in when customers choose dancers for the luxurious private rooms. Then again, it's only been a few days since Mia gave me a critique to earn more on stage.

Maybe it has started to work. Maybe it is really my time to shine.

As I climb the stairs, I try to convince myself that I deserve to be called back to the most expensive private room of all.

4

CALUM

I recline on the red velvet booth of Club X's platinum room, sipping a tumbler of expensive whiskey. My eyes are focused on the gleaming silver pole in the center of the room. Beneath it, low lights seep from the bottom of an elevated stage. The walls and floors all echo the same shade of dusty, iridescent red.

A low melody is pumped through unseen speakers, the sound brash against my ears. As I look up at the door, I see the top of the blonde's head through the open doorway as she climbs the last few stairs.

Anticipation slides down my spine. I take her in as she mounts the steps. Long blonde hair, blown out to fall over her slim shoulders in a gleaming mass. Tawny hazel eyes, high cheekbones, a pert nose, and a small slick of hot pink on her mouth. Her lips alone are an invitation, parting as she lays eyes on me.

My gaze slips down to the rest of her body. She wears a sheer white kimono, an iridescent black bikini underneath that, and tall silver heels. Her tits are pushed up, looking small but tempting. As she stops at the door to toe off her heels, she turns and gives me a glimpse of her long legs and fantastic ass.

She's a dead ringer for Honor. At another time, in another setting, she could be the delicate prima ballerina. The same one that broke my heart back when I was young and foolish enough to still believe in that fairytale.

She enters the platinum room quietly, tilting her head as she takes me in. "I'm Cerise." She swings her hips as she struts toward me, her eyes wide and innocent.

Like she doesn't work in this fucking club and make her money by grinding on strange men. Like she isn't working me right now, trying to figure out my weaknesses.

Her feigned innocence does something to me. It makes my cock hard, yes. But it also makes me think dark thoughts.

Violent thoughts.

My mouth tightens just a little. "You can call me Mr. X."

Her eyebrows lift just a fraction as she comes close to me, putting a hand on the velvet booth. She leans down, giving me a peek of her creamy cleavage. "You want me to dance for you, X?"

My cock stirs. Her tits are small and firm, pressed up by her bikini top. I drag my eyes up to her face, my voice erupting in a guttural rumble.

"Mr. X," I correct her sharply. "And yes. I want you on the pole."

She flashes me a smile. She turns, hips swaying, and heads back toward the door. "How long do you want me, baby?"

She presses a discreet button and her music comes on, sultry and low. She turns toward me, an eyebrow lifting. "Is this loud enough?"

I couldn't care less about the music, honestly. Chances are that if it was made in the last hundred years, I won't like it anyway.

I flap my hand, uninterested. "I'll buy all of your time tonight, Cerise. Just hurry the fuck up. I want to see you dance like you did downstairs. That's why I chose you."

Her cheeks stain hot pink. She glances at the floor for a moment. "You saw me dance on stage?"

As she asks, she starts moving toward the pole. Hopping onstage, she starts to approach it. I sit back, feeling my pulse pick up.

"That's right," I say. I try to play it cool as though she's not about to take her clothes off and try to make me horny. Sucking in a deep breath, I tell myself to relax.

She hops up onto the platform and starts gyrating her hips, running her hands up through her hair and down the front of her body. Her eyes close and then pop open for a moment, pinning me in place as she rubs the silky material covering her pussy.

Something about her expression, a heavy lidded innocence, really fucking turns me on. She's like a virgin giving off fuck me eyes for the very first time.

I know it's all a show. I know that it can't be real. But I let myself sink into the moment, let myself be swept along by the tide.

Cerise grabs the pole and swings around it, undulating her body. I tilt my head to the side and bite my lower lip. She climbs the pole deftly, leaning out and then letting her back bow until she touches the floor with her hands. She does the splits in midair, her kimono falling so that I can see her legs and her material covered pussy.

"Take off your robe," I order.

A little smirk appears on her face. She dismounts the pole by doing a roundoff, then gives me a sultry look. She unties her kimono slowly and then shrugs out of it, leaving her in the black bikini.

I take a sip of my whiskey, trying not to show how base my thoughts are. I'm excited by the slight curves of her hips as she dances before me. She bows before coming back up very slowly, never breaking eye contact with me.

Then she grabs onto the stripper pole with one hand and lifts onto her tiptoes. Her arm arches gracefully above her head. She leans forward, extending her leg behind me. I trace the curve as it lifts behind her.

When I saw her do this move before, I thought that perhaps she had some ballet training. But now I think it's more than that.

My lovely little ballerina is truly talented and well trained. The fact that Cerise is working here at Club X is a puzzle. She's been involved in a hardcore ballet program somewhere, I can tell. Unless she has recently quit, she is doing something very forbidden in the ballet world.

I sit back and watch her climb the pole again, hiding a smirk. Moonlighting here is a definite no no, whether her program explicitly says so or not.

The song shifts just as she pulls on the strings of her top.

"Cerise," I command. "Come here."

I pat my thigh. She blushes, climbing to her feet. Her

hips sway as she pads over to me. Her cheeks color again when she stands over me, leaning forward to push my shoulders back against the red velvet booth.

As she looks me right in the eye, I wonder how she manages to blush on cue. I know it's doubtless a manipulation of some sort. But I have to say, it's working on me. I can feel myself falling under her spell.

Especially when she straddles my lap and sinks down so that I feel the exquisite pleasure of her ass against my thighs. My instinct is to grab her, to take control.

I am always in control.

But I just ball my hands into fists and tense my whole body.

"You should be mine," I tell her, looking at her perfect little tits.

She puts her hands up against the booth behind my head. "I am yours, Mr. X. You can ask me for anything tonight."

I scowl. "What if I want you at my beck and call? Hmm?"

I raise a hand and push her hair off her neck. It's so fucking silky and soft against my fingers.

Cerise shakes her head. "I don't know."

She rolls her body, grinding against my cock. My eyes narrow on her face.

"I could be your patron. That's what all the girls here want, isn't it?"

Her brow wrinkles. "Too much talking. Not enough dancing. Don't you agree?"

I clench my jaw. I think she just found a polite way to tell me to shut up. Then again, she's pretty much dry humping me. I try to relax, try to focus on the softness of her skin, the gentle hint of rose that wafts off her neck, the warmth of her pressed against me.

It's almost like intimacy and just as addictive.

She looks me in the eye; I can see from this close that her eyes are tawny brown with green flecks. She presses her hands against my chest, biting her lip, and leans close to my ear.

I'm not sure what I'm expecting, but she just lets out the breathiest sound, the tiniest of moans. She grinds her body against mine as she grabs my hands and brings them to her waist.

"Fuck," I grit out. I'm surprised at how this girl has managed to turn me out. I lift a hand and plunge it into her hair, wishing more than anything I could pull her in for a kiss.

Of course, I can think of other ways that she could please me… My eyes are glued on her mouth, imagining her on her knees, opening those lips, sucking my fucking cock.

My cock is currently pressed between our bodies; each time she grinds on it or rolls her body, I come a little bit closer to doing something very, very wicked to my little ballerina.

"Tell me something," I whisper. "Do you know how much this turns me on?"

She blushes and grins. She undulates her body, rolling it against me, and cocks a brow. "Why don't you tell me?"

Instinctively, my grip tightens in her hair. She's so dainty as she rides my lap, so angelic and yet so fucking dirty. She gasps in surprise as I start to move against her, thrusting my cock up between our bodies.

She stills for the barest moment; I seem to have crossed one of her boundaries though she doesn't say so.

I take my hand out of her hair and return it to her waist, knowing that I could easily snap and take things too far.

I've done it before.

Hell, I've even done it at this club, in this booth. I've definitely gone all the way from kissing to fondling to being blown by a stripper.

There is something holding me back from Cerise, though. I don't know if it's the fact that she's obviously had ballet training or the faux innocence that she projects. Maybe it's her smell, a vague splash of rose but nothing too fake or flashy.

But I look into her eyes and something echoes between us. A longing, perhaps.

I wish I was the kind of man that she thinks I am. She probably just sees wealth and good looks when she looks at me.

But beneath that scarily thin veneer lies something so twisted and so dark that there is no chance at redemption. Not for me.

Cerise drags me from my thoughts by pushing up off my lap and sinking to her knees. She rubs her hands up and down my thighs, biting her plump lower lip and making eye contact with me. She lowers her head and kisses my thigh.

My eyes close for a second. Shivers of anticipation run through my veins. She's barely even touching my leg. I haven't felt this kind of crackling excitement since I was a teenager.

God, if Honor ever touched me like this, ever sat on my lap and ground against my cock, I—

I don't even know that I'm going to come before it's already happening. By the time I realize that my balls are tingling, it's already too late. I'm literally so surprised that I don't even warn her that I'm about to come. I don't say anything; my brain and my mouth are both too out of it to do more than whisper, "oh *fuck*."

The orgasm bursts over me and spurts out the tip of my cock, which twitches like it is fucking possessed. It's like a dam of pleasure has suddenly broken open. From the top of my head all the way down to my toes, I feel my endorphins pumping into my bloodstream, causing a moment of pure euphoria.

Cerise swipes her hand too close to my dick and gets a wet, sticky palm print. She looks at her hand, then looks up at me. Her eyes widen with genuine shock.

"Oh, Mr. X—" she starts, blushing furiously.

As if she's never seen it before. As if she didn't work for it, teasing me. As if she didn't cause it to happen.

I shut down.

"Move," I bark at her.

She scrambles back, standing up. My mouth twists into a grimace as I pull a card from my pocket. It's all black with a shiny stripper pole outlined in red. I force the card into her hands.

"Here. It's five thousand dollars."

I turn toward the door, ready to leave. My heart still beats like a drum in my ears.

"Wait, this is… for me?" she says, sounding a little taken aback.

I pause, looking back at her. "It's less than I make a minute. Take it."

Then I stride out of the room, leaving her standing there, mouth agape. I hurry out the club, pulling up my phone to text my limo driver. My hands are shaking a little as I step out onto the darkened street.

Damn. Despite my best efforts, I still went way too far. I turn and look up at the club, a nondescript building on a street full of warehouses. I see a window open a few floors up; faintly, I think I can make out a pair of wide hazel eyes staring back at me.

Cerise.

As the limo pulls up, I get in the back seat, not bothering to wait for the door to be opened. I feel vaguely dirty. But as I give the order to head home, I already know the truth.

I'll be back to visit her.

5

KAIA

"Shit, shit, shit," I curse under my breath. I rush up the broad steps that lead to the three story gray stone building. My eye catches on the sharp angles of the big picture windows against the overcast morning sky. The New York Ballet building is a monolith, taking up half a New York City block.

My left shoe is wearing dangerously thin. Even the newspapers I've shoved in the sole won't save this pair for much longer. As I rush up the stone steps of New York ballet, I make a mental note to spend a little of my hard earned money on a new cheap pair of flats.

I can see my ballet class gathering upstairs through the wide windows. I'm definitely going to be late. Tucking my head down, I push through the massive plate glass door, trying to calm my nerves.

Every ounce of my energy should be focused on this visit to the hallowed halls that I've dreamt of for so long. But a part of me is distracted.

Remembering with a shiver Mr. X's gaze from the

39

night before. Tall, dark, and handsome, he was the customer that every girl dreams about. He was so freaking hot, so demanding, and so *on edge*.

As I hurry up the stylized concrete stairs to follow my class, I bite my lip. There was a moment when Mr. X suddenly went stiff last night. Only a few seconds later did I realize that he'd... finished... It honestly surprised the hell out of me.

After that, he shoved a card carrying five thousand dollars at me and left abruptly. It all happened so fast that I just felt... confused, mostly.

It also made me wonder about Mr. X's life. Who was he? Aside from his money, I wanted to know more about him.

I can still feel his deep blue gaze on my body as I rush along.

I come up to the top of the stairs, seeing my class on the other end of the airy hallway, moving into the doors of the largest theater. I run to catch up with them, trying to look dignified in my gray sweater dress and heels.

I miss the door closing by half a minute. When I push through the dark doors and enter the back of the theater, my dance teacher and several stoic looking New York Ballet representatives take note.

I swallow and blush furiously, rushing to file into the rows of seats with the rest of my class.

"Hurry up," a silver haired man snaps at all of us. He is dressed in a light blue button up and dark slacks, but he has rolled up his sleeves and unbuttoned his top button. He's classically handsome and very in shape. I would put money on his having been a dancer at some point.

As I sink into the velvet seat, I notice that Eric moves to sit next to me. I blush and give him a little nod, but there is no time to whisper.

"I'm Basil Smith," the silver haired man announces, leaning against the wall of the stage. The stage behind him is dark, the curtains pulled tightly.

I try not to think of just how badly I want to be a featured soloist, dancing on point on this exact stage. I want it so badly that I can actually hear the applause of a ghost audience echo throughout the great hall; badly enough that sweat begins to break out on the back of my neck at the thought of looming interviews for the company.

"I am the main choreographer here at the New York Ballet. I'm joined today by Chase Gorley and Emma Rosenburg, who are on the NYB board."

He waves his hand to indicate the two people beside him. Emma is probably in her fifties and petite, with a dramatic sweep of shiny dark hair and an immaculate navy sheath dress. Chase reminds me of a lot of Club X customers; he is older than Emma by at least a decade, well dressed in a dark three piece suit, and carries a great deal more weight on his frame than anyone else in the room. He cocks his head, seeming unbothered by this, and studies all of us instead.

"We have brought you all here today as the first part of our interview process," Emma says. Her voice is high and reedy, her expression stern. "At the NYB, we want to evaluate each dancer on his or her strengths and see what they might add to our company. But just as important to the hiring process is making sure that all applicants get to know us and understand the unique and challenging environment of the company before continuing with the interviews."

Basil smirks a little at her words. "Yes. Thank you, Emma. We will be giving you a run down of the history of the New York Ballet as a company, followed by a dance class focusing on the rigors of the NYB."

Chase cuts in, his voice low and rough. "Only then do we start the interviews. And I have to say, we are selecting maybe five new dancers out of more than a thousand new applicants."

"Joining this company is very competitive," Basil agrees. "Only the creme de la creme need apply."

Emma glances at her slender wristwatch. "Can we move things alone, Basil?"

Basil gives her a look so cold, I swear I feel its icy chill all the way here in the back row of students. I glance over at Eric, arching a brow silently.

His lips twist into a tiny smirk. He rolls his eyes.

"Yes, thank you, Emma," Basil says, his tone dry. "The New York Ballet was formed in 1947, with a rather spectacular roster of dancers—"

A muffled scream comes from somewhere far behind the curtain that hangs heavy across the stage. It's a woman's voice, tinged with a French accent, growing closer as it rises in pitch.

"You bastard!" she bleats. "You absolute… fucking… bastard!"

Basil slowly turns toward the sound, his expression completely unsurprised. "Honor, darling! I'm holding a class here and we can all hear you."

That name gives me pause. Where have a I heard that before?

But before I can focus on that, it's swept away by muffled footsteps approaching the curtain.

"Let go of me!" Honor shouts. "I'm going to tell everybody about our little affair, Mikhail!"

The curtain moves like there is a scuffle going on just beyond it. Both of my eyebrows raise; the argument that Honor and Mikhail are clearly having couldn't be choreographed better if they tried.

Honor rips the black velvet curtain and stalks out on stage, shaking Mikhail off. She is lithe and blonde, dressed in a white leotard and a filmy white ballet skirt. She's followed by a desperate-looking Mikhail, his black t-shirt and jeans setting off his silvering dark hair. He glances at his audience, his lips twisting in a grimace.

"Let them all know!" Honor declares, sweeping her hand to indicate her audience. "Tell everyone what you just suggested when I told you that I was pregnant with your child."

Mikhail glances at us, shaking his head. When he finally speaks, his deep timbre is heavily inflected with Russian or Ukrainian.

"Don't," he warns her. "Don't make this public."

I can see Honor practically vibrating with rage. "No? You don't want me to tell everybody out here? What, are you afraid that word will get back to your wife?"

My eyes widen. I glance at Eric and see him mouthing, "oh shit!" to me. I nod. This is some really juicy drama, playing out right before our eyes.

"You won't get me to change my mind by telling a

bunch of ballet students. Just have a scrape and be done with it!" he roars.

My hand flies to my throat. My jaw drops. I could be wrong, but I think Mikhail just told his lover to get an abortion. There have long been whispers about what happens when a prima gets pregnant.

I mean, you basically have to decide if you want your career to end or you want to continue dancing.

A hush falls over the whole room when Mikhail shouts that. He clenches his teeth, looks at the audience, and growls at us. "Grow up, will you?"

Basil straightens his spine, looking back and forth between the tearful ballerina and the fuming Russian. He raises his eyebrows.

"Relationships between dancers and stage managers are explicitly forbidden. Mikhail, you are her teacher, for god's sake. And Honor, you should know better. You're a student, no matter how much you advance in the company. If I am reading this situation correctly…" He gestures to both of them pulling his fist in tight. "We have a big problem."

Honor lifts her chin defiantly. "I would say that we are beyond having a problem, Basil."

Basil shoots her a glare and then turns back to his audience. "I think we will have to reschedule this for another day." He glances at Emma and Chase, who look livid. "Will you please lead your class out of the theater? Mikhail and Honor, let's go to somewhere more private."

Honor shakes her head and storms off the stage. Mikhail casts a jaundiced eye over us as we are standing up, muttering to himself as he follows Honor.

As soon as we get to the theater doors, the whispers of my classmates burst to life. I hear, "Can you believe that she just outed them both like that?"

Then literally everyone is talking at once. I feel a tug at my elbow and find Ella there, giving me a wide eyed glance. She pats her elegantly pinned up hair as she wonders aloud.

"Could you imagine having the balls to sleep with the prima ballerina and then telling her to get an abortion?"

I shake my head vehemently. "No, I definitely can't."

Eric catches up with us, easily taking up my other elbow. "Holy shit. That was insane. I thought that they were both playacting at first."

As we are herded down the echoing hallway, Ella wrinkles her nose. "I've heard that one in three ballerinas undergoes an abortion before they retire."

I roll my eyes. "That can't be a real statistic. I don't know about you, but I was put on an IUD when I turned sixteen."

Ella purses her lips at me. "Aren't you a virgin?"

My cheeks flame red. I bow my head, my eyes widening. "I am not!"

A lie, yes. I'm ashamed to say that I've listened to my father's explicit threats about what will happen if I ever sleep with anyone before I'm married.

I'll kill him, Kaia. If any man talks you into being his slut, I'll string him up and watch him suffer.

I duck my head. If my friends had the slightest clue about my home life, they would probably stop talking to me. I finally moved out of his house six months ago, but not without his scorn.

You want to be independent? Fine. I've tallied up the expenses of raising you and putting you through ballet academy. Do you know how much you cost this family? Three hundred and twenty five thousand dollars, Kaia.

I swallow. Three hundred and twenty five thousand dollars is a lot of money… and now that I've moved out of his house, that's what I still owe my dad.

It's the only thing I'm focused on at this moment, other than dancing.

I hastily sneak a peek at Eric, who looks completely unruffled by Ella's revelation that I'm a virgin. He changes the subject, easing the panicked feeling in my chest.

"What do you think happens to Mikhail and Honor? Do they get fired? Or just get scolded?"

"Definitely fired. Ballet companies function with a level of trust. How can anyone at NYB ever trust either of them again?"

Biting my lip, I clear my throat. "That could be good for us, actually. I mean, that means more spots open up in the corps, right?"

Manon is just ahead of me. She turns her dark head at that, laughing cruelly. "Yeah, right. Let's be real here. Your chances of getting picked to be in this company are basically zero. You should focus on finding a job teaching ballet at some kind of school for crippled children or something."

My heart thumps in my chest.

Ella jumps right in before I can even really react. "You're just pissed because your pill popping mom is in rehab again. Get a fucking life, Manon."

Manon glares at Ella. "Back at you, Affirmative Action Annie."

"Die in a fire, Barbie bitch," Ella fires back.

"Watch where you—" Eric says.

But before he can even get the thought out, Manon stumbles as she reaches the stairs. For a split second, it looks like she's going to take a header straight down.

But at the last moment, Manon's friend Roxie reaches out and steadies her. Manon sends us back a superior look, tossing her head and click clacking down the marble stairs.

Ella's mouth curves into a smirk. "Entitled little priss. Anyway, let's talk about Mikhail's wife. Do either of you know who she is?"

I shake my head, absorbed in the drama. As we walk out of the New York Ballet, I'm just really happy that I have friends that will stand up for me.

6

CALUM

Checking my watch, I consider leaving Emma's office at the New York Ballet. I'm not accustomed to waiting for anybody, especially not for nearly fifteen minutes. I'm a firm believer that you teach people how to treat you.

Heaving myself up off the sleek leather couch, I glance around the well-appointed office. My movement alarms the little redheaded secretary, whose cheeks flame bright red as I approach her in the doorway.

She squeaks out. "Mr. Fordham, I'm sure if you wait for another minute or two—"

I brush right past her, in no mood for her attempts to stall me. "Move."

She stares after me for a moment, then hurries to catch up with me. "I just know that Mrs. Rosenburg is tied up with—"

A door down the hall in flung open with full force, several people spilling out of it all at once. I see Emma first, looking chic as ever in her dark blue dress. Beside her are her fellow board members, Chase and Mark.

In front of all of them is Honor, bursting out of the room like a bullet leaving a gun. She holds her dark head high but she's clearly sobbing, all but running down the hallway.

Seeing her gives me pause. It slows my steps.

What on earth is the prima ballerina doing running away in such hysterics?

Mark scurries after her, calling her name. "Honor—"

Chase notices me standing only twenty feet to his right. He snakes out a hand and catches Emma, jerking his head toward me. She looks at me, clearing her throat in a way that suggests she is embarrassed.

It's hard to tell with Emma though, as usual. Some combination of years of ballet training and Botox has wiped all expression from her face.

She flattens her hands against her fitted skirt and tucks a strand of hair back behind her ear. "Calum. I'm sorry, I was obviously…" She looks down the hall after Honor, taking a deep breath. "We asked you to come in for a reason, as you can see."

I don't know what reaction she's looking for, so I play my cards close to my chest. I shrug, endeavoring to keep my expression neutral. "I'm going to need some kind of explanation."

She and Chase walk down the hall toward me. I give them a look, folding my arms across my chest. Emma flashes me what passes for a smile and ushers me back to her office.

"Please," she says. "Discretion is very important at this stage."

Turning around and shaking my head, I allow myself to be herded back into her office. She slinks behind the sleek metal desk; Chase plops down his considerable weight in a chair opposite. I remain standing, staring at them both. "What's going on?"

Chase purses his lips, glancing at Emma. "We found out that Honor and Mikhail are having an affair." He gives me a flat look. "Not even really trying to keep it secret, either."

My eyebrows rise. My mouth contorts. "Wait, she's fucking him? Willingly?" I scoff disbelievingly. "He's so old!"

Emma and Chase exchange a look. Emma leans her elbows on her desk, giving a dour look. "Yes. Not only are they having an affair, but Honor says that she's pregnant with his child. The whole situation is horribly messy."

Chase grunts. "She told an entire class of ballet students all the sordid details too. Honor really made sure that there was no way to walk the information back."

Emma sighs, giving her head a tiny shake.

"What's going to happen to her?" I ask, frowning. Inside, I'm a mass of venomous snakes and white hot anger. But I keep a tight leash on it for now; this isn't the time or the place to vent my fury.

Emma frowns. Or at least I think she tries to. With all her facial fillers, I feel like I can't really tell.

"She and Mikhail are both fired. That's what has to happen here. I see no other choice."

I wonder to myself if this is the break that I needed to

get Honor to take me as a lover. I've lusted after her for years, having known her for well over a decade.

"We thought that since you and Honor danced together at ballet academy, you might like to weigh in on how we should go about replacing Honor," Chase says.

I cock a brow. "Don't you have two or three ballerinas ready and more than willing to step into her place?"

Emma lays her hands flat on the desk. "There is no obvious replacement. We assumed we had two more years to find someone with that *je ne sais pas*."

Chase looks at his wristwatch. "You'd better tell him the other problem too, Emma."

I huff a laugh. "Other than not having a star to lead your spring productions?"

Emma's mouth twists. "We are also down a stage manager."

My eyes narrow. "I'm sure that someone could be lured away if the money is right. I've been pushing for someone to replace Mikhail for a year now." I pause, tilting my head. "What about Stein? He seemed less than enthused about the Royal Ballet when I talked to him last year."

"He was already scooped up by the Paris Ballet," Chase sighs.

I lean forward. "You have tried whoever Stein replaced at the Paris Ballet, then? Who is it, Berger?"

"We were hoping that we would pull in someone closer to hand, actually." Emma gives a rueful little smile. "I know that it's been five years since you last worked as a stage manager—"

My eyebrows shoot up. "You're kidding. Are you

joking?" I give a startled chuckle. "You just finished telling me that you don't have any stars and you are essentially rudderless without Mikhail. Which, by the way, I specifically warned you both about."

I fold my hands against my stomach and sit back, angry that they would even bother to ask me.

"Look, Calum—" Chase begins.

I shake my head. "After I hurt myself dancing, I moved on with my life. I started Indica Tech. I started Indica Charity. The last three years alone, I've been insanely productive."

"We would donate your salary to your charity, obviously," Emma says.

"And a portion of the ticket sales as well," Chase says. He shoots Emma a glare.

I level them both with a glare. "You would be doing my charity a disservice, because my salary here would be just a fraction of what I normally earn."

Emma holds up a hand. "When you were a dancer here, didn't you have to pull out of a show at the end?"

I squint at her. "I was hurt doing a production of Sleeping Beauty, if that's what you mean."

She bobs her head. "And you never got to stage manage a production of Sleeping Beauty, as far as I am aware."

"No." I lean forward again, engaged. "Is that what you are offering as bait? The lure of doing something new?"

Chase smirks. "Yes. We would need you for Sleeping Beauty and Giselle, two of the hardest ballets to dance or direct. And not that it matters, but there would also be some other smaller showcases, I imagine."

I sit back, pushing my cheek out with my tongue. None of what they are saying moves me in the least. But a light-bulb does go off in the back of my head. "If I took the position, you would have to inform the other patrons of the transition, wouldn't you?"

Emma and Chase share a glance. Emma clears her throat. "I suppose."

I smile a little. "I'm interested in doing business with one of your donors. Jack Schwartz."

Chase raises his eyebrows. "We could… maybe notify all the patrons? I mean, it wouldn't be very hard to put together some sort of elegant engraved card or something."

"It would have to highlight how much I've given over the last few years and how grateful the company is for my continued good works."

"Of course," Emma says. "We'll state that we are very grateful to you."

I purse my lips. "I think that someone in my office will gladly put together a thoughtful reflection on my career and more importantly, on my charitable nature."

There is silence just then as Emma and Chase look at each other. It goes on for a little too long.

I drum my fingers on the table, trying not to be offended. "I need you two to agree that I'm known for my good works above all else."

"Of course," Emma says, eager to please me.

I stare her down until she flushes a little.

"Well?" Chase prompts. "Will you do it?"

My mouth flattens. I raise a finger. "I'll think about it," I allow. "And I do mean think. I have a lot to consider."

Emma looks vaguely pleased. "We would so appreciate it, Calum."

"We'll see," I say, leaning back and shrugging a shoulder. "But regardless of whether or not I take the job, I need something from you."

Chase rubs his hands together, smiling. "What's that?"

"Let go of all your dancers that are not ready to move up and take the spotlight." I stand, casting a serious gaze at them both. "Anybody that isn't hungry for it? Demote them to the corps or fire them. Clear the way for thirty or forty brand new dancers to step forward."

"Oh, Calum." Emma says. "I don't know…"

"It's not a request. I'll make the money you receive from my charity contingent upon that condition."

I suck in a breath, looking at my watch. When I look back up, they both have sour expressions on their faces. "If that's all, I have a thousand things to do."

Emma stands up, graceful as ever. "I'll walk you out, Calum."

"No need. You two should be figuring out how to tell those dancers that they are fired."

With that pronouncement, I head out of the office, closing the button on my jacket as I go.

My emotions swirl in the air around me, concussing me. But I can see one thing very clearly.

Me taking a bow as the audience raves, the applause so thunderous that I can't hear a single voice in the back of my head.

My lips curve as I head out the front door of the building.

7

KAIA

I stand in my attic apartment in Jamaica, Queens, trying to find the will to leave. My black kitty Exupéry meows and rubs against my leg. He is completely blind but usually seems to be in good spirits. No one else would take him in at the animal shelter so I did.

Kaia, keeper of broken things.

My face would go great on one of those Catholic saint candles that I so love to collect. I turn my head and look at my collection of candles, each looking stoic on its cylindrical glass form.

What can I say, they are cheap at the bodega on the corner. Plus, when I light them, it gives my apartment instant ambiance.

I scratch Exupéry behind his ears and sigh. Taking a deep breath, I stop double checking the contents of my backpack. Exupéry butts me with his head.

"I see you," I tell Exupéry. Kneeling, I scratch him under his chin.

Purrs burst from Exupéry's chest. My lips curve upward in a smile. He always seems enthused about everything I do, especially if it directly involves me petting him. He's been like that ever since he strolled up the attic stairs when I left the door open last summer. He doesn't mind how tiny my studio is in the least or how secondhand chic my attempts to decorate it are.

He doesn't even seem to notice the fact that he's blind, other than the occasional fall down the stairs.

I make eye contact with him as I gently scratch behind his ears. "I wish you could come to Hartford with me. My family would hate you, but at least I'd have a buddy." I scrunch my face up. "You'd be a welcome distraction, honestly."

Exupéry's tail twitches; he loves being talked to and petted at the same time. I pet him for another twenty seconds and then I sigh.

"Okay. Wish me luck."

Grabbing my backpack, I shoulder the straps as I start down the stairs. It's only a few blocks to the bus I need to catch that will take me out of New York City and all the way to Hartford. It's cold and overcast as I climb on the bus and find a window seat.

I text my father to let him know I'm on my way. Then I stare out the window, trying not to bite my nails as the bus pulls out.

The question of why my father summoned me home is heavy on my mind. Did I just wait too long between visits? Or is there a more sinister reason?

The scenery changes, though I'm barely aware of it.

The gritty concrete texture of New York soon gives way to the strangely empty echo of the highway that winds itself near the suburbs. At one point, there are no exits for miles, just dead grass and barren trees.

Then we're in Connecticut; only an hour and half from New York City, Hartford likes to play the charming country cousin to it's older, more glamorous sister city.

Outside, the suburbs of Hartford are entirely different than that of New York. The streets here are clean as a pin, the yards expansive and green, the houses are huge three story affairs made of brick. It's kind of amazing how much each house looks to the next.

I suck in a deep breath and get off at my stop, my heart hammering the entire three blocks to my parent's house.

I trot the last forty feet up the yard, ringing the doorbell on the off-white brick house. Out of the corner of my eye, I see ivy starting to climb a corner of the house.

My father hates ivy. One corner of my mouth lifts in the ghost of a smile as I wait for someone to open the broad oak door.

But as soon as it opens, my smile vanishes. My sister stands there in her dark blue Catholic schoolgirl outfit, her blonde hair pulled halfway up with a long dark blue ribbon. Her lips twist with humor as she eyes me, wearing jeans and a black sweater.

"God, you look wretched," she says. "As always."

I repress a sigh. "Hello, Hazel."

She rolls her eyes and leaves the door open, heading down the long hallway into the kitchen. Pressing my lips into a thin line, I step in and close the door behind myself.

Although I've just come from the blustery day outside, it feels colder inside. As I head in my sister's wake, I guess that Dad has been on a money saving kick again.

The heating is usually the first to go when he rages about how everything costs him too damn much.

It's a frequent complaint because the costs of heating a house of this size here in Hartford are significant.

I walk into the kitchen, bracing myself. But my father is nowhere to be seen. Instead, my sister sits at the kitchen counter, absorbed in her phone.

My mother turns from the stove, her eyes hazel lighting up. She brushes off her aprons and hurries toward me.

"There you are, Chickadee," she greets me warmly. She hugs me hard, kissing my cheek. When she pulls back, there are tears in her eyes. "It's been too long since I've last laid eyes on you."

I pat her cheek. "You look good, Mom." My gaze slides around the kitchen and dining room. "Shouldn't the cook be doing your job?"

My mother flushes as she steps back, shaking her head. She heads back to the stove. "Esmerelda was let go a couple of weeks back. Your father caught her and the new maid stealing." She clucks her tongue as she pulls oven mitts on. "I mean, can you believe the nerve of some people?"

My father usually discovers that his housemaids are treacherous once per season; it happened so often during my childhood that I could almost time it down to the week. I feel bad for the servants who are hired here, to put it bluntly.

"Well. It smells good in here," I say, changing the subject.

My mother blushes and smiles at me. "Thank you, Chickadee. We should be ready to eat soon."

Slipping my backpack off, I carry it over to the bar where my sister is sitting. I set my stuff on the ground and slide into a seat.

"How is school going, Hazel?" I ask politely.

She doesn't even look up from her phone. "Better than it did for you, I assume."

I squint at her words. She's almost certainly a worse student than I was. Ballet academies don't screw around when it comes to grades. Mine was no different.

"Girls, be nice," my mother says. "Hazel, we only have Kaia here once a month. Let's keep it civil."

Hazel looks up at me and sticks out her tongue. I flip her the bird and she immediately tells on me. "Mom! Kaia just told me to go fuck myself!"

"I swear, you two," Mom says, whirling around. "Quit it, both of you."

My dad's steps suddenly break the tension, sounding like thunder coming down the stairs. I bite my lip. Hazel smirks.

My mother tucks her hair behind her ear nervously. We all turn toward the doorway, waiting. Three little arrows, primed and quivering, just waiting for him to release us.

Eventually he stalks into the room, muttering angrily. Tall, blond, and heavyset, my father is dressed in khakis and a white polo. He rakes his hand through his thinning hair and glances at the three of us.

"That was the fourth call I've gotten that was prerecorded JUNK!" he declares. "I've told you time and time again, Serena. You sign up for these…" He makes a gesture. "These lists and then I'm left getting my fucking phone called twenty times a day! It's fucking ridiculous!"

My mother doesn't even blink at the accusation in his tone. "They are the worst. I'm sorry, honey."

My father hikes his belt up, shaking his head. "I'm not dealing with that shit anymore, Serena. You can't expose us like that."

My mother nods, as if he's giving her sage advice. Before his barb even lands, he's already swinging his gaze around to Hazel and me. "Why are you dressed so casually, Kaia? In this house, we have a dress code."

I struggle to keep my feelings off my face. "I didn't know, Dad. I'm sorry."

He takes a couple steps closer. "Your sister and your mother are wearing skirts. I expect you to dress up like a woman when you want to come to dinner here."

This is entirely new since the last time I visited, just over a month ago. I swallow, bobbing my head. "Yes, sir."

My mother hastily turns to us with a platter of roast chicken and vegetables clutched between two potholders. "Why don't we sit down and eat?"

My father gives me a look as I stand up, shaking his head on the way to the formal dining room table. The table is long and glossy, laid with an extensive place setting for each of us, undoubtedly my mother's doing. Dad sits at the head of the table and my mom hurries to set the chicken down in front of him. Hazel and I take our places across from each other as he clears his throat and starts to carve.

My mom rushes back to the kitchen, retrieving several more dishes. My dad serves himself first, then Hazel. My mom sets a perfectly poured pint of beer at his place, then scurries to her seat.

My dad takes a bite of his food, seeming to forget that my mother and I are yet to be served. I stand and move to grab the platter of food. My dad growls at me, his mouth still full.

"Manners, Kaia!"

Hazel smirks at me, picking up her fork and putting a piece of chicken in her mouth. It takes my father another minute to serve me and my mom tiny portions of chicken and vegetables.

"I'm trying to help you both out here," he says, passing our plates back. "You both tend toward having fat asses. You guys both take after Serena's mother, who was herself practically a fucking cow. She was disgusting."

I glance toward my mother. I've never seen my mother bigger than a size two except when she was pregnant. But she just smiles benevolently down the table at my father, like he's really doing something great for her.

"Thank you, Robert. You always look out for us," she says. She glances around the table. "All of us should be very thankful."

Hazel has a piece of chicken hanging from her mouth when she mumbles, "Thanks, Dad!"

"Thank you," I echo quietly.

I look down at my plate, eying the tiny portions with a silent sigh. No sooner have I sliced a tiny piece of chicken off and popped it into my mouth does my father begin.

"When do you graduate again?" he asks, putting an elbow on the table. He spears a huge bite and chews it with relish.

"At the end of January."

"And when do you hear back from New York Ballet?"

My cheeks turn pink. "I don't know. I haven't gotten my audition date yet. There are a lot of factors, like how many more people they have auditioning after me."

He points his fork at me. "That's not good enough, Kaia. I need a date."

I swallow, dropping my eyes. "I'll try to find out, Dad."

"Good. I don't want to have to ask you again," he grunts.

"She is probably too busy with her social life to even pay attention to something like an important deadline," Hazel says cattily.

I huff a laugh. "Social life? Have you never seen how much I practice? There is barely enough time left over for me to sleep."

My dad fixes me with a glare. "I don't like sarcastic comments or snark in my house, young lady. Now apologize to your sister."

I give Hazel a dead-eyed stare. "Sorry."

My father isn't finished, though. He sets his fork down and leans in. "I would hope that you would have some fucking manners by now. I've spent almost twenty years and hundreds of thousands of dollars on your education and training as a dancer."

My neck heats. "Yes, sir. I plan to repay you every cent."

Everyone goes quiet. The idea of me earning that much money in my whole lifetime does seem absurd, on its face.

"Unless you have a check for the whole amount, I'm not interested. And I know that you will never have that kind of money. I mean, look at yourself, Kaia. You'll never be worth anything to anyone outside of this family."

My cheeks burn. He's right, of course. It does seem impossible.

I sneak a glance at my mother. She is chewing quietly, looking at her plate. No help is forthcoming from that quarter, not that I'm the least bit surprised.

My dad clears his throat and shoots me a glare.

"You're using the wrong goddamn fork. Did I not send you to cotillion and spend my hard earned money on you learning basic table manners?" He shakes his head, disgusted. "You should be a lady, like your sister."

I arch a brow at Hazel. She smirks at me, piling her fork full of potatoes. "Yeah, Kaia. You should at least try, even if we all know you'll fail. You can't help the fact that you suck."

"Don't say suck at the table," my mother corrects Hazel stiffly. "Kaia hardly ever comes home. Why don't we all change the subject to something more upbeat?"

My father, ever the drama queen, stands up to make his point. "I'll talk about whatever I damn well please, Serena. I put food on the table and clothes on the backs of everyone present."

My mom gives him a soft smile. "Of course you do, honey. Thank you for all that you do for us."

Hazel and I mumble thank you as one.

My father sits down. "You're welcome. Just the other

day, I was telling the guys in my foursome at the golf course about how much I do for my family. I said that you had all found me and thanked me within the last few days. Doug called bullshit, and I had to set him straight."

He shovels food in his mouth, talking anyway. "I said Doug, just because no one is thankful for what you provide doesn't mean that the same can be said about yours truly. Maybe my family is just better at showing gratitude than yours is."

I school my expression into one of interest. But underneath, my guts churn. This is exactly why I don't come home if I can help it. It always plays out the same way.

My father makes crude remarks. My sister eggs him on. And my mother supports it in the most non-confrontational way she can.

I do the best I can for the rest of the visit. That means I nod when I'm supposed to agree and only fill in details when asked. I revert to the person I was years ago, back when I still lived here full time.

I try to blend in with the wallpaper and not draw attention to myself. My father and Hazel shoot spiteful comments at me. I try to dodge them and not let the barbs hurt me.

That's the only way I know of to get by in this house.

At last, as the sun starts to set, I get ready to leave. My mom hugs me hard. Hazel makes some snide comment about how I'm putting on weight.

It just makes me really, really tired.

At last, I go over to hug my father. It's important that he see me as a doting daughter; anything more than that is considered rebellious.

"Bye, Daddy," I say, kissing him on the cheek.

He grabs me by the shoulders, staring down into my face. "You had better ace your audition with New York Ballet, Kaia. I haven't supported you for this long just to have you falter when the goal is within reach."

My eyes widen. I blink convulsively. "Yes, sir."

"I mean it," he says, giving me a sharp shake. "I won't have you taking some position with some far away place. You have trained for too long and cost me too much money to just blow it. You had better be the best damn ballerina they have ever seen. Or else."

The menace in his tone gets heavier the longer his sentence goes on. My eyes fill with tears, but I won't let them fall.

"Yes, sir."

He waves me off like I've displeased him. I grab my backpack and I'm out of the front door like a rocket. I'm almost out of the yard before I hear my mother's voice.

"Kaia!"

I slow, then turn back. She stands in the doorway, wringing her hands. There seems to be something that she wants to say.

There always seems to be something left unsaid with her. Several seconds pass as she tries to make up her mind about what she wants to say.

"Mom, I have to catch my bus," I say.

Her lips twist with a hint of bitterness. She looks down and shrugs. "Good luck on your audition, sweetheart."

I suck in a deep breath, my eyes filling with tears again. "Thanks, Mom."

She waves, looking so desolate and sad. I've long since

learned that I can't help her; she loves this life that has her ensnared, keeps her shackled to this godawful house.

Turning, I start walking toward the bus stop, my tears just now beginning to fall.

8

CALUM

"Sir, please. Be still so I can work on this knot." Hugo, my extremely patient physical therapist, pushes his hands flat against my bare back.

I open my eyes a slit. I can see myself reflected back in the mirrors that line that walls of my private gym. Lying on my stomach, I have a pained expression.

"Go on," I grunt, closing my eyes once more.

Hugo presses his hands against my flesh, rubbing small circles with his fingers. He comes to the knot again and his massaging only intensifies.

It hurts like a bitch as he works his hands over the knot, trying to loosen it.

"I can tell you're thinking about the knot," Hugo chides. "Remember, you should think calming thoughts."

I sigh and turn my head away. Hugo has been my physical therapist for almost six years, ever since I tore the anterior cruciate ligament in my right knee.

That's an injury that no dancer ever comes back from; one that saw me, at age twenty two and half, hurt and unsure of my future. With the help of hindsight, I'm glad that I got injured. It spurred me on, made me figure out how I was going to feed myself and keep Lucas in ballet academy.

But at the time, I thought my life was over.

Hugo finally finishes torturing me, patting me on the shoulder. "Okay. You can get up."

I turn myself over, grimacing and rotating my shoulder in its socket a few times. I glance up and see my reflection again.

Painted across the flesh and muscle of my chest, just to the left of my heart, are two tight white clusters. Once upon a time they were bullet marks, each entering my chest just shy of piercing my heart.

Now they are healed, the skin gone from pink and tinkered to white and shiny.

I hop up off the table and grab a black t-shirt, pulling it over my head. Hugo is already folding the table up and moving it back to its out of the way spot.

I bob my head. "See you on Tuesday, Hugo."

Hugo smiles. "I look forward to it."

He vanishes out the swinging doors to my gym. I roll my neck and rotate my shoulder again, still feeling stiff. Then I walk over to a rack of free weights, picking up a twenty pounder.

As I begin doing curls, the doors behind me swing open again. This time it's not Hugo but my brother Lucas.

And he has a displeased look on his face.

"Where were you?" he asks, annoyed.

I roll my eyes and focus on the weight. "You'll have to be more specific than that if you actually want an answer.

His fists tighten. "You know what I mean, Calum. You said that you would be at the Indica Tech board meeting this morning. I was counting on your vote."

Setting the weight down, I turn my head toward him. "Just do whatever you want to do, Lucas. The world isn't waiting around for you to get approval. The sooner you learn that, the better."

A muscle flexes in his cheek. "If you were just going to say that, why didn't you do it earlier? This project has been moving at a fucking snail's pace for months."

I suck in a breath. "You're supposed to be my second in charge. That means that you can do anything you want with the company. I'm the only person with the power to veto you. What more could you possibly want?"

Lucas shakes his head. "You're such an asshole."

I trot over to the wooden bench where my water bottle is, taking a sip. Checking the time, I am glad to see that it's almost eight at night.

The time which I can go back to Club X. I've been waiting for this.

"Is there something that you wanted?" I ask my brother distractedly.

He pushes his tongue out with his cheek. "Who is she?"

I cock my head at him. "I'm sorry?"

He makes a gesture with one hand, opening his palm to the sky and flapping it closed several times. "You've been avoiding work lately. The only time you do that is when you have your eye on some new girl. So who is she? Is she a ballerina or is she one of your whores?"

I shoot him a baleful look. "Get fucked, Lucas."

He chuckles, his expression reminding me of our father. "So she's a pro, then. God, what happened to you that you turned out so fucked up?"

I turn cold as ice. "Lucas, get the fuck out of my house."

Lucas doesn't get to judge me for the women I sleep with.

He eases back, holding up his hands. "I just came to tell you that you have a message at the answering service that's from Anita. Apparently it's been there for some time."

I look down at my fists, which closed tight at the sound of her name. "I know."

He rolls his eyes. "You should answer it. Or at least listen to it. Jesus."

I keep my expression blank. "Are you done?"

"You're a dick today," he huffs. He turns and disappears out the swinging door again.

I turn and look at myself in the mirror. I look like a little boy, clothing his water bottle, all mad at the world.

Walking toward my reflection, I hurl the water bottle. It hits the surface and explodes, distorting my image for a moment as the water runs down the wall.

Inside I'm writhing with anger, absolutely furious at the fact that Anita even had the fucking nerve to reach out. Not only that, but she obviously called my brother when no response was apparently forthcoming.

Her using Lucas really turns my stomach all over again.

She should know better. Then again, she's a snake.

How can I expect a snake not to poison everything within its reach?

The only other option is to tell my brother exactly how I got Anita to take us in after our parents died… and that'll happen as soon as hell fucking freezes over.

I close my eyes, struggling for control. I learned so much of it in ballet, perfect control of my physical being.

But mental control…

That's something else entirely.

I open my eyes as Club X wishes back into my consciousness.

Cerise in right there, at the top of my mind.

I'm going to make her mine tonight, no matter how much it costs. And then I'll be so distracted that all thoughts of Anita will flee.

Growling to myself, I turn and start to walk out of the gym.

9

KAIA

Thud, thud, thud.

My heartbeat is so loud that it almost drowns out the music.

I'm onstage at Club X, on my knees in the middle of the stage, listening to the last notes of my song. The top of my bikini is somewhere behind me; the bottoms are just in front of me. Whistles and cheers come from the audience; my face heats as the music shifts.

Climbing to my feet, I gather all the cash I can carry, making sure I pick up my suit at the same time. I run off the stage and dump everything down on a tall bar table put there for just that reason. As fast as I can, I rush out onto the floor. I see several men wave me over, raising their black plastic cards at me. My eyes rove over them, trying to pick between them.

One of the guys pops up, grinning. He's blond and young, his Harvard sweatshirt and acne-spotted cheeks dead giveaways. He leers at me as he comes over, waving his black card. "Hey! I want a lap dance from you. I have a room…"

I smile lightly. He seems pretty drunk. But half the guys in here are the same. "Sure. Lead the way."

I grab onto his arm to stop him from literally running. He flushes at my touch and slows it way, way down. I strut my stuff into the back, where the private rooms are located.

Okay, rooms might be overselling the place a bit. They are small black booths with room for no more than three people; I notice that the camera that points into the room follows us.

I push him down on the hard bench, feeling strangely loose. It's rare to get someone my age as a customer. Maybe just knowing that he's very human and visibly shaking helps me relax.

I press a button by the door and take his black card, sliding it into a slot. His choice of music begins to play, some seriously raunchy rap.

I smile and begin to dance for him. "What's your name, sweetie?"

He bites his lip, his gaze hard on my breasts. "Mike."

He reaches out and grabs me around the waist. Instinctively I push him back, shaking my head. "That's not how this works. You don't touch me."

He rolls his eyes. "Come on. We both know that you're going to get on your knees and suck my dick. Just go ahead and do it already. There's no need to wind me up first."

I paste on a smile but stop dancing. "I think you have the wrong idea. We don't do that here."

I turn my head and start to pull his card from the door. When I turn around, he's coming right at me. "Don't be a stuck up bitch. We both know you want it."

He unzips his pants and flashes me his penis, which is laughably small. He arches his eyebrow, as if he's daring me to touch it.

Before I can even push the hidden panic button, a big burly security guard is already behind me. "Everything okay in here?"

I step backward, out of the booth. "I think it would be best if this guy left."

"Wait a second!" the young guy protests. "I want what I paid for!"

I turn and walk out of the back area as quickly as I can. Unease settles around my shoulders like a cape, prickling me. My mouth quivers.

It's not that I'm afraid what would have happened back there. The management keeps their eyes on everyone and everything. If I were to believe Mia, they keep a lookout for people trying to cut them out of profits.

But for stuff like this?

I'm beyond glad that they are looking out for me, no matter what their motivation is.

I stop in the middle of the hallway, giving myself a hard shake. *This is part of it,* I chide myself. *This is exactly what you signed up for when you took this job. Now get a hold of yourself!*

I paste a smile on. Blowing a deep breath out, I start moving again. Before I even make it all the way back onto the floor, the manager Sam comes to find me.

He doesn't even blink at the fact that I'm scrambling to get my mind straight. He just sniffs, adjusts the waist of his black pants, and looks at me through jaundiced eyes. "You were good onstage. You do that dancing ballet thing and the whole room goes nuts. It's one of the best acts here."

My cheeks turn beet red. "Oh. Uh, thanks."

He seems not to notice, or maybe it's just that he doesn't care. "Mr. X is here again."

I look up at him, my eyes going wide. "He is?"

He nods. "Yup. He just headed up to the platinum room with a bottle of our most expensive whiskey. He asked that you entertain him again."

My heart gives a little flutter in my chest. "Oh! Well… I will head upstairs now."

Sam holds up a black pair of pointe shoes. "He wants you to wear these."

My cheeks flame scarlet as I pluck them from his grasp. "Thank you."

I climb the stairs, my heart in my throat. A giddy little voice in the back of my head is babbling about how Mr. X is here to see me.

But no. He's not.

I have to remember that he's here to see Cerise, who's more confident and self-assured than me by a mile. It's a show I put on, a diversion.

No one is interested in plain little me and it's best that I remember that.

Swallowing tightly, I climb the last step to the Platinum room. Lifting my chin and planting a demure smile on my face, I see Mr. X's dark figure through the open doorway.

He's a little more disheveled this time. His tie is loosened at his neck, his dark suit jacket is thrown aside casually. When he sees me, his eyes light up like twin sapphires, sparkling dangerously.

I step into the room, closing the door behind myself. "Hello, you."

He smirks, his eyes dropping to take in my whole body. "I couldn't stay away," he husks out.

The deep timbre of his voice gives me goosebumps. I press a button near the door to turn on my music. It's low and rhythmic, making me sway along.

I smile and bend down, making quick work of swapping my stripper heels for pointe shoes.

When I finish tying them on, I stand, giving them a test. I lie and then do an arabesque. The slippers fit perfectly. Because of the variability of sizes and shapes, it's nearly impossible to guess what size slipper someone is by just looking at them.

"How did you know what size to get?" I ask, walking across the room in slow steps.

He smiles coolly. "You ask too many questions, beauty."

I stop when I'm inches away from him, tossing my hair and posing. "Did you miss me?"

Mr. X leans forward, looking me right in the eye and running his fingertips oh so lightly up my knee toward my hip. I sink my top teeth into my bottom lip.

I should push his hand away just as I did to the boy

downstairs. I should put up hard boundaries and stick to them, be firm like Mia taught me.

Yet I don't. I just let him touch me, throwing back my head and swaying my hips to the music. He slides his hand around my back and gives me a tug.

I have to take a little of my power back. So I pluck his wrist up and drop it by his side. "You're just supposed to sit back and enjoy this," I say sweetly.

His eyes narrow on my face and his lips twist. But I shut him up by moving closer, putting my legs just inside his, and lifting my leg high over my head. His breath all leaves him in a soft grunt as his eyes travel up my body.

"Fuck," he mouths quietly. He reaches down to adjust his cock, leaving his hand on his lap. "You're killing me, Cerise."

The rush of emotion that I feel when he tells me that is addictive. I let my leg come down and kneel, my knees going wide as I straddle his lap.

He grabs my ass and pulls me down, grinding his cock between us. His eyes darken with need.

"God damn," he grits out.

I lean forward, placing my hands on either side of his chest and pushing him back. As I push him back, he lifts his hips, grinding against me again.

I know I'm not really meant to get turned on. But he does briefly brush his cock against my pussy in a way that makes me tingle. Without thinking I let out the softest moan, pressing my hips down as I gyrate against his lap.

"Oh fuck," he whispers, plowing his hand into my hair. He bucks against me, his eyes hard on my face. I bite my lip as my hips jerk against him; it's hard not to close my eyes.

"That's it," he says through clenched teeth. "Right there, beauty. Don't stop."

I feel a damp spot growing on the flimsy piece of fabric between my thighs. I can admit it, I am very excited right now, ready to tear my clothes off and…

And what?

Let him penetrate me?

My cheeks flush. I need to chill out before I end up accidentally having full blown sex right here, right now.

I don't want to stop, don't want to slow it down. But I slow the rolling of my hips, opening my eyes.

Mr. X is watching me closely, his hips lifting in time with my own. "Are you sure you want to stop?"

His question makes me blush all the way down to the roots of my hair. I suck in a breath and push off his brawny chest, trying to play it off. Admittedly, I'm a little wobbly as I step away from his lap.

I turn around, letting him look at my ass. "I thought you might appreciate a different view."

He glances up at me, his gaze tightening on my face. But after a second he shrugs a shoulder and reaches out to touch my ass cheek. "Your ass is perfect. Do you know that?"

I blush as I bend down to touch the floor, using my hands to push up onto my tiptoes again. Mr. X seems to like that, shifting his weight and bringing his hand back to the crotch of his slacks.

"Tell me you'll be mine," he says, his voice gone to gravel. "Dance just for me. Let me be your patron, Cerise."

I sway along with the music. "You'll have to give me a better name to call you than Mr. X." I say, smiling.

He smirks. "Sit on my lap right now, beauty, and I'll whisper it in your ear."

I grin and take a seat on his lap, twerking rhythmically. Instantly his hands land on my hips. His cock is pressed against my ass. He groans and leans forward, whispering in my ear.

"You can call me Calum."

I reach back and knot my fingers in his nape, steadying myself as my hips work. "Oh, Calum…" I let out the breathiest moan.

"Fuck, I'm going to—"

He thrusts almost violently against my back a few times then lets out a roar. I feel his cock twitch against my skin. A small wet spot soon spreads out between us. The sound of him finishing is somewhere between fascinating and terrifying, gratifying and sobering.

"Fuck me," he says, chuckling against the bare skin of my shoulder. "That was…"

He trails off as I swallow and get up off of his lap. I'm not sure how to talk to him just now.

It's not that I didn't want him to… complete. It's more that I don't want him to expect it every time he comes to see me.

I'm not sure how to bring that up to him, so I busy myself taking off my ballet slippers instead.

He sprawls back against the leather booth, throwing a hand over his eyes. "I know that it's frowned upon to come when you're touching me."

I set the slippers on the leather bench where he's

sitting, walking to my pair of heels. What am I supposed to say?

That I wanted him to come?

I did. But that doesn't make it legal. It was prostitution, technically.

…right?

I slip on my heels without saying anything. He sits up, eyeing me. "Where were you trained, Cerise?"

I fumble with one of the straps to my heels. My heart starts beating loudly in my ears. "I'm not sure what you mean."

He produces a shiny black card, holding it up as a present for me. When I stalk over to grab it, his free hand comes up and ensnares my wrist. "Yes, you do. It was somewhere good, I can tell you that much. Was it here in New York City?"

My eyes widen. Under no circumstances am I about to tell him a damn thing about my personal life. That's dangerous territory.

"That's way more than you need to know. Why don't you leave something to the imagination?"

I pluck the card from his hand, my lips pasted in a frozen smile. He lets it go, his gaze narrowing on my face.

In the next moment, he sits back and shrugs. "Okay. How about you give me a phone number, then? I want to be able to call on you when I need you."

Mia's voice erupts out of my throat. "When I see a signed contract, you can get me a phone."

Calum arches a brow. "Is that so?"

I start back out of the Platinum room. "That's right."

His expression darkens. "You sure you know what

you're signing up for? You won't work here. You will only dance for me, beauty. Whenever and where I want it."

Swallowing, I nod. "I know."

I turn and flee down the stairs, my head full of contradictory thoughts.

I just gained a patron… but I won't sacrifice my privacy to keep him, if I can help it.

CALUM

Two days later, I'm standing by the studio's only window, frowning out into the inky blackness. Basil is in the opposite corner and between us are the current group of dancers. Basil leans down close to one ballerina, his black-clad body looking rather like a knife.

"You can leave," he tells her. He looks her up and down, his expression severe. "Your pirouettes are disgraceful."

The twenty ballerinas and dancers surrounding her don't stop moving, even when she bursts into loud, sloppy tears. Basil turns on her classmates, sighing silently. He watches their movements like a hawk.

I fold my arms across my chest, my eyes tracing the dancers' arms. I can see that half of the dancers here are lacking in the natural grace with which Honor was so proudly blessed. There are also a lot of nerves right now.

Even though the class has been instructed to impress Basil and not worry about me, I am getting plenty of looks.

Not because I'm handsome. Not because I'm rich, though I'm sure that's part of it.

No, they are looking at me because it was announced earlier today that I will be directing all of the spring productions.

And I won't be pulling a single punch.

"Stop!" I call out, shaking my head. I look to the corner where the piano player sits. "Stop playing."

The room is abruptly silent. All eyes are on me. I walk to the middle of the room. Several dancers back away, making room though I ask for none. I look around, pushing my cheek out with my tongue.

"This is going to be the last combination we're going to do tonight. I would suggest that if you're going to impress me, the time to start doing that would be right the fuck now."

I look to the piano player, signaling him with one hand. He starts playing the same notes, a lively Chopin number.

I draw myself up, starting in first position. As I execute each move, I call out to the class. "Ladies! You start with a this, a this, into a this. Then you'll do four pirouettes and finish with a big jump. As wide and exaggerated as you can."

The ballerinas nod, most looking tense.

"Gentlemen! You should begin by the wall…" I head for the wall and the dancers get out of my way. I ready myself, starting in first position once more. "Move, move, move. Pirouette, rond de jambs, arabesque, hold it… for… as… long… as… you… can."

I finish with a little bow. The male danseurs look a

little shocked that they are being asked to do an arabesque, which is traditionally considered a ballerina's move.

But if they are to be compared to the ballerinas, I need to see them do the same thing.

I start clapping time. "Come on. Let's go. Ladies, line up. One and two and three and…"

I watch the ballerinas and dancers twirl and hold their poses for the next few minutes. I'm looking for strength and beauty, grace and expressiveness.

When the last note is played, I call to the piano player. "Thank you. You can go."

I turn my eyes on the class again, frowning. "You can go too. Rosters of those staying with the company will be posted tomorrow morning." I dismiss them with a wave.

The dancers all take off at a run, whispering amongst themselves. Soon the room is empty but for Basil and me. I lean down and rub my right knee, feeling the ugly surgical scars.

Basil walks over, nodding to my knee. "Giving you trouble, is it?"

I snort. At the moment, I'm in real pain. It arcs down from my knee like white hot sparks, burning and tight. "Something like that."

He jerks his head over to the long wooden bench. "Let's sit, then. You can tell me what you thought."

I move stiffly over to the bench and drop on it, rubbing my knee. "You had to know that last batch was all but useless. We've seen five classes today, ranked best to worst. And that was definitely the dregs."

He plunks himself down, plucking his water bottle up.

He looks thoughtful as he squeezes a little water into his mouth. "They weren't great."

I scoot down and raise my leg to lie out straight. Almost instantly, the burning pain subsides and leaves a low level throb. I'm so relieved I could almost cry.

"There were some hopefuls in the first two classes," I say, screwing up my face. "But there weren't any that had it, if you know what I mean. I was looking for someone with star quality."

Basil nods absently. "Someone to replace Honor."

"Yes." I rotate my shoulder, reminding myself to have RehabGuy look at it later. "When are you going to have the American Ballet Academy and the School of American Ballet try out?"

His eyebrows lift a little. Usually the company deals with that, not a patron or a guest director. "I think sometime next month, maybe."

I roll my head over to him. "No. Make arrangements. I want people in here to audition tomorrow morning."

He blinks. "Excuse me?"

I heave myself up off the bench with a groan. "Make it happen, Bas."

As I walk away, he explodes.

"This isn't your private tech company, Calum! You have everyone here running around like fools, desperate to please you. I'm telling you now, that won't last."

I roll my eyes. "I get shit done, Bas. I don't have enough time in the day for all the niceties. I just tell people what is expected of them and fire them if they can't or won't comply." I lean over, scoop up my duffel bag, and sling it over my shoulder. Then I glance back.

"Someday, you'll meet some girl that makes you fall to your knees. And she won't behave according to your rules." He favors me with a twisted smile. "Then we'll see who is crying uncle."

I shake my head, walking toward the door. "Love is for people who are foolish enough to have hearts. Meanwhile, I'll be here tomorrow morning, bright and early. So you'd better start sounding the alarm right now, because there had better fucking be a shitload of dancers for me to judge when I get here."

"Calum—" Bas calls. But I hit the doorway, checking my phone.

I grumble a little. There are still no emails or missed calls from Club X. That means that they are still processing the rather lengthy contract that Cerise and I signed, officially making me her patron.

I drum my fingers on my thigh, then take an abrupt right turn into the men's locker room. I run through a quick shower and change into a fresh white collared shirt and black pair of slacks. By the time I walk out of the changing room, I've settled on a plan.

Since Club X can't offer me what I want, I'll look elsewhere. As I push out the great glass doors and head into the cool night air, I quickly head for my waiting limo.

I climb in the back, not waiting for the driver to open the door. Tossing my gym bag aside, I look up toward the partition, which is rolled down.

"Sam, take me home. But pull up outside the Continental instead of into the parking deck. I want someone to make me a drink."

My driver nods, already absorbed in pulling the car out of its spot.

It's only a short drive to the enormous skyscraper where I own the penthouse. I slide out in front of the Continental, a sleek little cocktail bar that opened last spring.

Since the grand opening, I have spent many meetings and cocktail hours at the dimly lit, wood-paneled bar. It's menu is brief but memorable; the customers are either healthy people that either live in the area or people who want a really, really fancy gin and tonic. The uber rich mingle with the models and actresses and cocktail snobs.

It's a fantastic place for hooking up, basically.

I stroll up to the door of the bar, swinging the door open. Hushed lighting greets me. The walls are all dark wood, lined with soft pink velvet banquettes. I cast an eye over the bar as I approach. It's an old airplane wing standing before towering shelves of colorful glass liquor bottles. There are probably fifteen seats at the bar and only ten of them are occupied.

Adjusting my cuffs, I slide into the first open seat I see. The bartender sees me and recognition lights his face. He heads over with a cocktail menu and a coaster.

"Good to see you, Mr. Fordham. What can I get for you?"

I don't even have to think about that. "An old-fashioned."

He bows his head. "What kind of whiskey do you want in that?"

I sit back in my seat. "Elijah Craig or something comparable."

"Right away," he says, reaching for a rocks glass.

I turn my attention toward the rest of the bar, where a large group of young girls in high end dresses are now gathering. I watch as one girl orders. Her friends notice me and a couple of them blush, making eye contact.

Like I said before, it's pretty easy to pick up a hot stranger here. The bartender puts my drink down, but I'm busy narrowing my selection. Sipping my drink, I look back and forth between a blonde and a brunette.

The brunette makes up my mind by getting her martini and taking the empty seat next to mine. She takes a sip of her drink, looking at me out of the corner of her eye.

I lean closer, smirking. "I'm Calum. And you are… not a regular here, I'm guessing?"

She blushes, shaking her head and smoothing her hand down the front of her little black dress. "I'm Olivia. And no, I'm from Philadelphia. I'm just in town for my friend's bachelorette party."

My eyes narrow, my smirk grows more pronounced. It couldn't be more perfect if I'd written her lines out for me.

I pick up my glass, nodding to it. "Have you had their old fashioned yet? Everybody should have one once."

Olivia smiles coyly and tucks a strand of her curly hair behind her ear. "Why no. Do you want to order me one, Calum?"

Twenty minutes of chitchat and two drinks later, I'm pulling the brunette down a dark hallway in the back of the bar. She kisses me first as I elbow my way into a dimly lit bathroom with a dazzling floor to ceiling mirror. She isn't a very good or very experienced kisser, her hesitation obvious.

She giggles, tipsy and enthusiastic, as I press her against the back of the door. Her lips are warm and rubbery under mine. I can feel her hand shyly exploring my belt.

Without speaking, I back her against the sink. Here too I am reflected as I unbuckle my belt.

The brunette rips my shirt out of my slacks, her eyes dark with need and full of hunger. I feel nothing except a faint throb from my cock. I push her down to kneel on the floor as I free my cock, staring at myself in the mirror.

If I'm honest about it, watching myself get my dick sucked is most of the reason why I always come here when I'm looking for some action.

She puts my cock in her mouth. It feels good, although she does keep nipping me accidentally.

"Cover your teeth," I murmur, dropping my head back. "Use your hand."

I guide her hand to the base of my cock. She comes up for air, breathing hard. "Maybe you should just fuck me?"

Suppressing an eye roll, I yank her to her feet and turn her around, pushing her against a wall. I roll on a condom then take her panties down to her knees. Stepping close, I pull up her dress as press my cock against her ass.

I still feel nothing, although I do have a hard on. Then again, I almost always have a hard on, so…

Running my fingers along the curves of her ass and down to her pussy lips, I turn my head. The only way that I can get off is by watching myself in the mirror, essentially watching porn of myself.

I fit my cock to her entrance and thrust in deep. She makes a strangled sound. I stare at my reflection, unable to stop the hatred from surfacing. I fuck this girl with all the vitriol I feel for myself.

Fucking useless, I think, thrusting deep.

She holds on and moans. I punctuate each thrust with a thought.

Fucking.

Waste.

Of.

Space.

I grit my teeth, hammering my cock home over and over again.

There are a thousand reasons why you're all alone, I think, glaring at my reflection.

You're.

So.

Fucking.

Weak.

Look at you. You're broken. You'll always be alone.

I'm not even making a half-hearted attempt at paying attention to the girl. My eyes are laser-locked on my reflection, sneering.

"I think I'm going to—" the brunette husks out. Then her pussy spasms around my cock. She lets out a strangled scream as she comes.

I'm nowhere near finishing. And yet, I pull out of her body, stepping back. It's a matter of seconds before I get the condom off my dick.

"I fucking hate condoms," I mutter.

The brunette, whose name at this point I can't even vaguely recall, blushes. "Well, I'm clean if you—"

Disgusted, I toss the condom in the trash and start zipping up. "That's vile."

Her eyes widen as I leave, banging the door open. "Wait—"

But I'm done.

Done with condoms, done with sketchy bathroom fucks. I exit the back way and walk through the echoing marble lobby, my mouth a grimace.

I need to see Cerise again.

I know that she has the right combination of tits and ass and hazel eyes. She'll make me come without even touching me.

And until I can fucking blow my load, I'm going to be an absolute fucking terror…

11

KAIA

As I step out onto the stage of the New York Ballet, my feet and legs tingle. I can't keep the grin off my face. Ella is right behind me, finding a spot and sitting down to put on her toe pads and pointe shoes.

I bend down, putting my own toe pad and shoes on. Mine are in terrible shape; I definitely should've worn a newer pair of shoes. But a new pair of shoes wasn't in the budget this week.

These have to last four more wears.

I straighten, looking at the empty theatre. From where I'm standing, it's easy to imagine the roar of excited applause, the hot lights, the other ballerinas watching from the wings.

I blow out a breath. Ella looks up at me. "Are you okay, Kaia?"

I wrinkle my nose. "Honestly, I never thought I would make it this far. My goal this whole year has just been to get to this moment."

"Sit down and put your shoes on, boo. You look like a ghost. Get your shit together."

I wince, but she is right.

She seems to be murmuring something to herself. I plunk down beside her and retape my third and fourth toes, pulling a face as I look at my feet.

All dancers have calluses on their feet. But ballet dancers have it the worst, especially ballerinas. I slip on my toe pads and put my pointe shoes on, fastening them.

"Be comfortable," I whisper, shooting them a glare.

Ella glances over at me as she gets to her feet. "Can you believe we are here right now, about to audition?"

I spring to my feet, looking at the other twenty dancers. Everyone is practically vibrating right now. The nervous energy is almost palpable.

I stretch my right hamstring. "Can you believe that they fired the company's prima ballerina and most of the corps? When I saw that they were auditioning for forty spots…"

Ella smiles coolly. "We need those spots."

She takes first position, doing a series of plies.

I look at her, dead serious. "God, what if we actually get called back?"

Ella pulls a face. "Of course we're going to get called back. We dance literally eight to twelve hours per day, six days a week. We deserve it."

I flush, looking down. If I did the math, I am absolutely sure that I dance literally every minute I wasn't asleep or commuting. But I don't say any of that.

"Yeah," is all that comes to mind.

Ella stands up straight and adjusts her dark blue

leotard. She nods toward the back of the theatre, where a dark haired woman in a blue skirt suit and a short blond man in a white tank top and black capri tights approach us. The man claps his hands loudly; he's obviously a teacher, because he seems used to holding court.

"Hello, ladies and gentlemen," he says, coming down right before the stage. "I am the head instructor here, Basil Smith. And this—"

The woman cuts in stepping forward. "I'm Emma Rosenburg. I'm the head of the board that oversees every action undertaken by this company."

Basil gives her a long look. "Yes." He turns his attention to the group on stage. "Your director is running late, it seems. He's not polite enough to let anyone know about his tardiness—"

"Basil," Emma chides.

He climbs up on the stage, looking annoyed. "But never fear. Emma and I will be judging. Also, I think someone is filming this audition." He looks behind him, searching for how that is happening.

"What my colleague is saying is that you should be your absolute best self, starting right now." Emma backs away from the stage, hurrying to find a seat in the fourth row.

An older woman comes out on the stage and finds a seat at the piano.

I can't quite feel my legs because I'm so full of nerves.

You'd better make it in New York, my father's voice sounds loudly in the back of my head.

Pushing that thought down, I try to concentrate. This is all about me, here and now. There's no room in my head for Basil or Emma, Ella or my dad. It's all about me, my talent, my precision and skill.

I just need to keep reminding myself of that.

"Line up four across," Bas barks, clapping his hands. "Girls in the front, boys in the back. Let's move, people." He narrows his gaze at all of us. "God, try to act like you've all been in a chorus line before."

I scurry into place beside Ella, my heartbeat going wild. Deep breaths. *You can do this*, I say to myself.

Basil waves at the accompanist, who starts playing Tchaichovsky. He looks at everyone flatly. "Let's start very simply. Pas de chevalier to point. Tendu side in fondu. Close to fifth position. Okay?"

No one says anything, so he sighs. "And one, two, three, four…"

Never in my entire life have I arched by arms so high, moved so quickly, or stretched my leg back quite so elegantly. The moves are accomplished in the blink of an eye.

I look to Basil, who raises his eyebrows at the group. "Good. Again."

I do it a second time, finishing with a perfectly shaped arabesque. After I'm done, my heart pounds in my ears.

Am I actually… good at this?

It feels like I'm killing it so far.

"Okay, now I would like to see something more complex," Basil says. He walks to the back of the stage, starting in fifth position. Then he proceeds through a combination with a pirouette in the middle and ending with a grand jeté. "And five six, seven, eight. One, two, three, four. And five six, seven, eight…"

My heartbeat rises. Every single move he executed is flawless, not that I expected any less. Toward the back of the theatre, the door swings open and a man enters.

But I'm too focused on what I'm doing to pay him any mind.

"Let's go!!" Basil yells, clapping. "On my cue. One, two, three, and—"

The first line goes. I cue up right behind, trying to focus my attention on the moves.

"One, two, three, and—"

Like a puppet come to life, I am suddenly smiling and dancing. I keep my movements smooth and easy, doing a complex pirouette with several turns and then leaping across the stage. My legs carry me far. I land right in center stage, beaming, and lift my arms.

This is it. This is the feeling that I'm supposed to have, I think to myself.

That's when I suddenly make eye contact with him.

Eyes as dark blue as sapphire, and glittering just like two gems. Dark hair, grown a little overlong, shoved back from his face. High cheekbones, a jawline that could cut diamonds, a cruel yet perfect pout.

And that big, rugged, sinful body that I know all too well. The very same one that I dreamed about riding last night.

Mr. X is here.

And he is glaring right at me.

Oh *god*.

All my worst fears, all in one place. The person who judges me is the very same one who I've been all but fucking at Club X. The same person that already inquired if I had training from a good ballet school, knowing perfectly well how taboo that is.

My smile falters, my arms droop. All the blood plummets to my feet.

"Get out of the way," Bas snaps at me, waving his hand. "Next line, keep going…"

I manage to break his gaze and force my feet to carry me to the side of the stage. It's only when Ella reaches out and mouths, "Are you okay?" that I realize I'm trembling.

I bob my head woodenly. There is no real reason to alarm Ella and I certainly do not want to draw any more scrutiny to myself.

"Let's go again!" Basil calls out. "Same combination. Same lines. Let's go, first group!"

I line up in the second group, automatically taking fifth position. I raise my arms and begin with the rest of my group. Somehow, though, the magic that I felt only a few minutes ago has disappeared like smoke. Now every leg lift is harder, my grand jetés less exaggerated. Even my pirouettes seem to take forever.

Everything slows down.

Knowing that I'm being watched by those searing deep blue eyes just makes all my steps clumsier, all my lifts less impressive. I can feel myself powering down.

Is this really happening to me right now?

I finish the combination a good four steps after the rest of my group. Basil looks me up and down, pushing out his lips in a dissatisfied expression. "Do better," he warns.

I nod at him quickly, glancing out at Calum and Emma. Neither has much expression on their face. But Calum's gaze is burning a hole through the middle of my torso.

I scurry to the side of the stage, turning away from that gaze. Ella comes to stand next to me, raising a brow as she glances back at our audience.

"Do you know him?" she asks in a hushed whisper.

I take a breath, trying not to panic. "Who?" I ask, all innocence.

She narrows her mahogany gaze at me. "Obviously I'm talking about the sexy guy standing next to Emma. He's been glaring at you since he got here."

Not wanting to risk a glance over my shoulder at Calum, I just shake my head. "Nope. Never seen him before."

The lie burns as it leaves my mouth. Ella gives me hard look, knowing that something is up. But Basil claps his hands together, drawing her attention away.

"All right! Now it's time for your solos. I know that you weren't expecting to perform them quite so soon..." He shoots a cool look off the stage. I don't know what that's supposed to mean, but he quickly moves on. "Anyway, we need to see them now. You can line up right here and give the pianist your music. Then we'll start."

For a long second, nobody moves. It's a sea of inexperienced, wide eyed kids, all looking to the others for reassurance. Then Ella clears her throat, grabbing my hand. "Right away, Basil. We're ready to go with our solos."

My cheeks flush as I let her pull me over to the other side of the stage. Everyone hurries to line up after me. Basil smiles coolly at Ella.

"Thank you. Are you ready?"

Ella nods, dropping my arm. She turns to the pianist and

tells him to play a selection from Romeo and Juliet. The woman starts playing the beginning notes of the piece and Ella strides to a starting point, lifting her chin and smiling.

As I watch her dance, my stomach drops. She's better than most of the dancers I know, better certainly than me.

Who isn't better than you, little mouse?

I swallow against the whisper of my dad's voice. Blinking rapidly, I glare out off the stage, where Calum is staring me down.

I won't cry.

I can't.

This is my only chance.

Ella finishes her routine, bowing elegantly. There is a smattering of polite applause. Basil nods and turns to me. "Next?"

I clear my throat, turning to the pianist. "Would you please play the beginning of the second act of Giselle?"

The accompanist arches a brow at my choice of music; I've chosen one of the hardest pieces to perform for my solo.

She starts playing and I hurry to my place at the back of the stage. My heart is beating like a drum in my ears. It's almost hard to hear the music over it.

Luckily, I have practiced this exact piece thousands of times. Using nothing but muscle memory, I smile as I parade out, doing a dizzying number of pirouettes as I dash across the stage. All time stops. Everything just becomes about my breath, my limbs, my feet. Making sure I push myself into the next movement.

The music is very upbeat and I smile along as I do the

arabesques and grand jetés that are required. I am moving too quickly to see any one particular person.

But when I come to center stage and pause for a moment, Calum is still standing there, staring at me like I am an insect to be crushed.

Holy shit.

The judgment I see written all over his expression is terrifying. I turn, pirouetting once more before I complete my three grand jetés off stage.

Somehow, I land slightly off balance coming out of the pirouette. Then I'm forced to try to overcompensate as I carry that force into the first jump.

And everything slides off kilter, suddenly. My timing is off; my feet don't seem to land in the place that they should. My legs are heavy, my arms near useless.

By the time I finish my solo, I can feel tears brimming in my eyes. I still turn and curtsy to signal that I am done. And there is a scattered bit of applause. I look toward Basil, my heart thundering in my ears.

He looks at me, his mouth twisting like he just ate something bitter. "Your ending could really use some work, honey."

My heart wrenches. The sob that has been barely contained in my chest flows up and out of my throat.

I crumple, turning and running offstage.

I finally had my big chance… and I fucking blew it. Openly sobbing, I run away from the stage, pointe shoes and all.

CALUM

I climb out of my limousine on a busy street, pulling my coat closer and blinking into the blinding streetlight. Night has fallen and the city is teeming with the late night crowd, especially this part of Hell's Kitchen. There are a lot of bars, strip clubs, and massage parlors right around here.

I round the corner, heading into a dark alley. Music throbs as I jog down a few steps that lead to the entrance of Club X. A bouncer sits by the club's heavy front door, his sharp gaze taking me in. I've shifted to a black hoodie, black leather jacket, and black jeans, There is no trace to indicate my wealth or status.

Then again, I suspect he's used to seeing that, working the door here.

"Password?" he asks.

I stare him down. "Apricot."

He slides off his stool and rolls the door aside. Music pours out of the doorway. As I step through into the hallway, the floor glows faintly, leading me back into the depths of the club.

Rap music grows louder and louder until I'm awash in it. I turn the corner and see the main floor of the club: the black tables sprinkled here and there, the sleek black bar, the center stage and pole, a naked redhead grinding on it.

I look around, my gaze landing on one of the managers lounging at the bar. As I stalk over to him, he straightens up, his eyes widening just a bit. He sniffs several times. Between that and his pupils as dilated as dinner plates, something tells me that he's on a shit ton of coke.

"Cerise," I bark at him.

He starts. "What?"

I step closer to him, folding my arms across my chest. "Cerise. Where the fuck is she?"

His adam's apple works convulsively in his throat. "In the back, man." He looks at me, glassy eyed. "Are you going to cause me a problem tonight?"

Ignoring his question, I reach inside my leather jacket, pulling out a fat wad of hundred dollar bills. I roll a few off, slapping them down on the bar. "I want to see her in the Platinum Room in two minutes. Got it?"

He snatches up the cash, squinting around the room. "I'll go get her for you."

I'm already walking away, headed for the staircase. My heart is pumping overtime.

I didn't actually think that it would be so easy to find her. I haven't actually planned what I'm going to say to her.

Running up the last couple of stairs, I push the door open to the Platinum Room. The black leather booths and the shiny bronze stripper pole beckon. As I take my customary seat, I try to quell my excitement.

Everything that I want is within my grasp. All I have to do is play my cards just right.

I see the flash of ash blonde first. Then her hazel eyes and her pouty mouth. Her whole body comes into view, wearing a black string bikini and platform stripper heels.

Her expression is just short of open rebellion. That little bit of fire actually gets me going as much as her tits or her ass.

I like that she thinks she can actually fight back against me. That makes my cock hard.

She reaches out to flick a button at the door and then eases it shut. Her music starts playing a woman singing in sultry voice over hip hop music.

Cerise walks straight up to me, folding her arms across her chest. "What are you doing here, Calum?"

I look at her, almost radiating anger as she stands above me. A smirk plays on my lips. My fingers itch to touch her, but I resist.

"I came to see you. Apparently you haven't signed the paperwork making me your patron yet."

Her eyebrows fly up in surprise. "What? Why would I sign those? After you go to the board of the New York Ballet with what you know—"

I give my head a little shake. "I'm not going to do that."

She stops, looking confused. "What? Why not?"

I reach out, brushing my fingers along the line of her outer thigh. She jumps at my touch, scowling at me.

Ah, I love her reaction.

"My goal is not to embarrass you at work, beauty," I husk out. I trail my fingertips up, toying with the strings holding her bikini together.

She swallows nervously. I have to suppress a grin. It's not quite time to let her see me in my full colors.

No, there's an amount of wooing yet to be done.

"My goal has never been to tarnish your reputation. Rather, it has been about getting what I want."

I smooth my hand around the side of her hip. Then I make eye contact with Cerise as I slowly move my hand around to cup her perfect ass. It's firm and warm to the touch.

She swallows again, blushing and dropping her gaze. "And what is it that you want, Calum?"

I can't help but grin at that. "I want you, beauty."

She loses patience. "I don't understand! You have me! You summoned me, here I am. You can use any girl here however you want! I think you know that better than I do…"

I shake my head slowly. "I don't want to have you here. I want to have you wherever I want, whenever I want." My smirk returns. "That's why I wanted to be your patron in the first place. But now I can offer you something unique in exchange for… your time."

I toy with the string on one side of her bikini, tugging on it gently. She bites her lip, frowning just a little.

"Come again?"

I begin to pull her down to straddle my lap. She doesn't like it and resists a little.

I enjoy watching her squirm. I enjoy forcing her down roughly even more.

Once she is sitting astride me, I grab the back of her neck and pull her close.

"The New York Ballet," I whisper in her ear.

Her entire body freezes up. She pulls back, scanning my face. "I don't understand."

I give her a smirk. "I'm the new stage director. If you want a spot in the ballet, Cerise, you just have to ask me."

Her eyes narrow. She starts to stand up, but I put my arms around her waist and grind into her body.

"It's Kaia," she says softly. "Not Cerise."

I already knew that, of course. Kaia Walker. But still, I enjoy the concession when she offers it to me.

"I'm offering you a role, Kaia." I brush my fingertips across her jaw, threading my fingertips into her hair. Then I grip her hair hard for just a moment, long enough to remind her of who is in control here.

She glances up at me, her hazel eyes wide. She's flushed and breathing hard, seeming to take my every word at face value. There is something naked and almost touching in her naïveté.

I drop my voice to a whisper. "I saw you dance today. You were good. With practice, you could be great." I tilt my head, studying her lovely face. "I can give you private lessons, beauty. In exchange for being on call for my needs."

She blinks. "And what are your needs?"

I grind my hips into hers again, biting my lip. "Devilish and deranged, for starters. I would be able to fuck you any time, any place. But I think we would both enjoy it, Kaia."

She sucks in a deep breath, her cheeks flushing scarlet.

"I don't... I don't think I'm the one you want, Calum. I'm... not..."

She breaks off, shaking her head.

I renew my grip on her hair, making her gasp. "I think you're exactly what I want, beauty."

She shivers convulsively, her gaze clashing with mine. "You don't understand. I'm... I haven't been with anyone before."

"I'm going to be your first patron?" I ask, smirking a little. "I think you're going to be fine."

She groans, frustrated. "I'm trying to tell you that I'm a fucking virgin, Calum! Okay? I haven't fucked anyone before and you seem to want... something else." Her nose wrinkles. "Someone else."

My jaw drops for a second. I stare into her eyes, floored.

How...?

Why...?

What the fuck?

Did I hear her right?

The girl that made me come in my pants the very first time we met is a fucking virgin? The very same one that I have wet dreams about two or three times each night?

I let my gaze drop to her tight little body. Her perfectly kissable tits, her ass that I want to bury my face in, her undoubtedly magical untouched pussy...

"Holy *fuck*," I say. Because what else can I say? "Are you serious right now?"

Kaia bites her lip, blushes, and looks me deep in the eyes. I know that she's a stripper. I know that it's to her benefit to lie about something like this.

I know that any man would literally kill to be in the position I am in right now.

I know all of that. But when she whispers *yes* in that breathy tone of voice…

I believe her.

I slide both of my hands to her hips, giving my head another shake.

"Oh, beauty," I whisper. "Don't sign the Club's contract. We'll work out a private deal, just between the two of us. I'll teach you everything I know, in and out of the bedroom. We'll do every decadent, dirty, hedonistic thing I've ever even dreamed of."

She scans my face, as if trying to decide if I really mean what I say.

"I'll still be able to dance as part of the New York Ballet, right?" She sucks in a breath after she says it, holding it in.

I tighten my grip on her hips. "Yes, Kaia."

She bites her lip. "And you won't… like, tell anyone? About our arrangement, I mean."

I solemnly shake my head. "No. It's honestly just as bad for an administrator to be seen sleeping with a dancer as it is for a dancer to have a side job. Either one spells trouble if they were found out."

Kaia blows out a long breath, then looks at me. "Then… yes. I'll do it." Her cheeks blaze bright red. "Should I… do you want me to get undressed right now?"

I'm taken aback by her red-faced offer. I tilt my head, looking at her for a moment.

I don't know her very well at all, but I'm starting to *get* two things about her.

She lacks self-confidence and she *really* has low expectations for how she should be treated. Whether I should read into that or not, I have yet to decide.

It honestly probably doesn't bode very well for me. But she is so, so fucking hot.

Not to mention untouched…

My lips quirk. "No, beauty. Save it for the next time we're alone."

She gives me a small lopsided smile, but I can see the gears turning behind her eyes. She's trying to figure me out, just as I am her.

I lean forward, kissing her collarbone. I like the way she shivers at my touch; I like the way her skin gets goosebumps everywhere I touch. I like the way her breathing becomes uneven as I suck on her collarbone hard enough to make a mark.

Kaia pushes away from me after a minute and slides off my lap. "I should go. I have to talk to management, I guess."

My lips twitch. "Let me take care of it. You can just go home and get a good night's sleep. Tomorrow, you'll get a call inviting you to the NYB."

She blows out a breath. "I guess… thank you, Calum."

That draws out my most wicked grin. "Don't thank me yet. I promise that you'll earn your keep, beauty."

Her eyes widen. But instead of asking me more questions, she turns and rushes off, heading down into the club.

13

KAIA

"I still can't believe that all three of us are here," Eric says. He glances at himself in the mirrored wall of one the New York Ballet's rehearsal spaces, stretching his hamstrings out at the barre.

He's not wrong. For this morning's class, we have more than thirty people crammed into a relatively small dance studio. "I wonder how many people they let go and how many people they brought in," I murmur, looking around.

Ella is in splits on the ground. She throws her hair back and purses her lips at him. "I can't believe that Manon got called, too. It honestly makes me wonder what the instructors were thinking."

Sitting down on the floor to do butterfly stretches, I giggle at that. "You're terrible."

Manon turns from where she is warming up at with a glare. She does a rude imitation of my giggle. "Hehehe!" Then her lips twist bitterly. "I hope you all get hit by busses on the way home."

I give her a skeptical glance, shaking my head. Ella doesn't miss a beat.

"Manon, how's your mom's pill addiction doing? I heard that she flunked out of rehab for the third time in a row."

"Shut the fuck up," Manon snaps.

Ella gives her a thumbs up, smiling sarcastically. "You're still a bitch!"

I roll my eyes. "You two really get each other going."

"Look," Eric says, jerking his chin to the entrance of the rehearsal space.

The room quiets as Basil and Calum stalk in, already looking pissed. Basil wears dark spandex leggings and a dark tank top. Calum wears a pair of loose gray pants and a plain white t-shirt.

Prowling around the room already, Calum runs a hand through his dark hair. He's magnetic without saying a word; I can't take my eyes off of him.

"Is that one of our directors?" Ella whispers to me. "He's so fucking hot. He must work out a lot."

I nod, not looking away from Calum. I watch his gaze swing around, observing the room. He pauses when he sees me, a smirk appearing on his face for just a second. His sapphire eyes pin me in place and sear me through.

"All right!" he calls. "I need your attention, everyone…"

Basil claps his hands, the sound they produce thunderous. Everyone falls silent, directing their attention to the front of the room. I realize just then that my heartbeat is going a million miles an hour.

Just being in Calum's presence makes my stomach flutter oddly and my cheeks feel hot.

"I'm Basil, or Bas. You all know me from your auditions. I'm the main choreographer here at NYB. Three facts about me: I'm married. I live in Florence three months out of the year. And I like seeing a lot of lift and extension in dance. Okay?"

He pauses. There are a couple of tentative yeses mumbled through our class.

Calum puts his hands behind his back, appearing pensive. He walks by the row of students on the other side of the room, observing each one as he paces. "I'm Calum. I'm your stage director for the spring season. I'm going to cut to the chase." He smiles coldly, his eyes taking in everyone in the room. "As you can see, we've brought in thirty five of you to replace the departing cast. We only need twenty or twenty five of you. So this first week will be a test of sorts. I'm going to be separating the wheat from the chaff. Dead weight gets cut."

My eyes widen. I glance at Ella. She looks at me briefly, her mouth tightening.

Calum pauses, looking at Basil. "Are you ready to get this class started?"

Basil cocks a brow. "I suppose so. Meesha, are you ready?"

He turns to the accompanist, a dark skinned young woman sitting behind the upright piano. Meesha nods. "Whatever you would like for me to play, Bas," she replies in heavily accented English.

"Some Schubert," he says, lifting his hands. She begins

to play and Basil calls out to the class. "I hope you are all stretched out. Let us begin with simple plies."

I clamber to my feet and position myself at the barre. Bas claps in time to the beat, explaining what to do.

"First position. And one, two, three, four. Now raise, two, three. Down, two, three, four. And lie, two, three, four... deeper, two, three, four."

His words are meaningful of course, but they sort of fade into the background for me. For almost my entire life I've had someone chanting those words or something nearly identical to me. The teachers were old and young, black and white, male and female. It really doesn't matter to me in the slightest.

No, I'm not worried about him. It's Calum that I catch myself looking at in the mirror. It's Calum who soon completes his circuit around the room. "That's the worst line I think I've ever seen."

He points to a ballerina at one of the barres set up in the middle of the room. "Straighten your back, stick your ass out, find your fucking center of gravity."

The ballerina turns red and plies again, prompting Calum to shake his head. "You're going to have to do better to earn your place."

An unsettling silence fills the room for a minute. He frowns and moves on, stopping a few places down at a young Latina dancer. "I'm not sure you've ever done this before. Work on your posture. Extend your arm..."

The ballerina smiles anxiously and tries to emulate what Calum says. He shakes his head. "No. No! Stop, everyone stop. Look at me."

He shoos away the dancers standing next to the Latina, taking first position.

It's the first time that I've ever considered whether or not Calum actually knew what he was talking about, if I'm honest. But he is pure grace and holds the perfect form when he plies, slowly going through the motions. His arm arches, his legs bend, his back is straight as a steel beam.

My jaw drops a little. I had no idea that Calum was so versatile; honestly, from the looks of him, you would think that he was an elegantly shaped football star, not a dancer.

What a way to prove me wrong. Calum finishes the pose and then steps away from the barre, eyeing everyone. "Just so there is no confusion, I can do pretty much anything I ask you to do. So when I say bend back further or hold the position longer, I know it is possible."

Bas seems unimpressed. "Thank you, Calum. Now, if we may resume class? And one, two, three, four…".

It's hard to tear my eyes away from Calum. I'm focused on not fucking up something so simple as a plie in front of him, though.

He casts his gaze over me and frowns. "Straighten your back. Push out your tailbone." Mortified, I immediately turn red and try to correct myself. Calum lifts a brow. "Are you kidding? Act like you're been in a fucking dance studio before."

Tears well up in my eyes. I look straight ahead, desperate not to cry in front of everyone. At the same time, the class keeps moving through the plies.

Everyone is perfectly at attention. Calum keeps his harsh gaze on me for a few seconds. "Not good, but better."

Then he turns his head, scoping out another dancer, and moves on. The whole class moves on, through plies and arabesques and fouetté turns. The entire time, Calum struts around the room, unhappy with each and every silhouette that he sees.

I'm the only one that gets multiple nasty comments, though.

"Your feet are all wrong. You should move nimbly instead of looking like Frankenstein's monster."

"No, no, no. When I say execute a grand jeté, I mean really go for it. Don't be fucking hesitant. The audience has no time for you to be timid."

He stops me mid-class, staring at my feet. "Go get a new pair of shoes from the shoe room. This is the New York Ballet, not a dance recital put on by medieval peasants. I expect you to dress like you belong here."

My eyes well up with tears. Nodding, I run out of the room, making it out of there before I burst into tears. I miss almost ten minutes of class because I have trouble finding a pair that are just the right size.

When I sneak back in, Calum shoots me a glare. I gulp and rejoin the rest of the class.

By the end of the afternoon, I'm barely keeping it together. To be fair, several dancers do start crying or get upset and leave in the middle of the class. But after my mini-breakdown, I stay resolute.

This is my shot at greatness. I'm not going to blow it for anyone, especially not Calum.

When class is finally over, Basil claps for the remaining dancers present.

"Very good! Tomorrow we start learning a new

routine," he announces. Sliding a look at Calum, he purses his lips. "And my colleague will probably go a little easier on you tomorrow. Right?"

Calum looks unimpressed, stalking away to where he set his water bottle down. I expel a long breath and look around for Ella.

She's already shouldering her duffel bag. "I have to go. I have a doctor's appointment that I'm almost definitely going to be late for."

Nodding, I blot my eyes. "See you tomorrow."

She flashes me a hard smile and hurries out the door.

I turn toward my bag and find Eric there, waiting patiently. "Hey." I tuck a strand of my hair behind my ear.

My cheeks start glowing a hot pink when I think of Calum standing just on the other side of the studio, watching me.

Eric shoulders his bag, smiling at me tiredly. "I thought I would walk you out today."

My blush spreads to my neck and my chest. I have a thing for Eric, but I also have made some promises to Calum. "Oh." I glance back but Calum isn't even in the room anymore. Letting out a sigh of relief, I nod. "Yeah. Let's go."

I snag my own bag and hurry out of the studio, licking my lips apprehensively. Sure enough, when I step out of the room, I see Calum. He's leaning against the opposite wall, his arms crossed, his expression bordering on hateful.

And he's glaring right at me. "Kaia? A word."

My eyes widen. I glance helplessly at Eric, my heart beginning to pound. He shrugs.

"Want me to stay?" he asks quietly.

Do I want my crush to hear what my strip club patron has to say to me? Definitely not.

"No," I say, forcing a smile. "Thanks anyway. I'll catch you later."

Calum stays put for a moment, watching Eric with a disapproving expression. The last stragglers from my class walk past me; soon we are alone in the echoing hallway.

Calum pushes himself off of the wall and strides over to me. I look up at him, losing my breath. He's so much taller than I am and he still has well-defined arms and sculpted physique that one would expect of a dancer.

He stops when he's a foot away. But I can practically feel the heat radiating off him like a torch.

He casts a glance down the hallway, where Eric went. "You can't fuck him. You know that, right?"

My eyes widen at that. "Who said anything about that?"

His searingly blue eyes find my face and tighten on it. "I'm telling you right now. You won't fuck him, not while you're…" He pauses, looking around to be sure we are not overheard. "Under contract. I forbid it."

I shake my head, rolling my eyes. "You can't forbid me from anything."

He clenches his water bottle so hard that it groans. "Don't test my patience on this, beauty. You'll see. I can do whatever I want, to whomever I want to do it to."

I cross my arms and cock my hip. "Of that I have exactly zero doubts."

He digs in his duffel bag and produces a note, wrapped around a hundred dollar bill. "Be at my home address tonight at seven. Don't you dare be late." His gaze drops down to my body, his lips twisting. "And wear something that turns me the fuck on."

With only those instructions, Calum sends me a last little glare and starts walking down the hall.

"Tonight?" I call out after him.

But he doesn't stop, doesn't acknowledge that there was even a question asked.

I crumple the money and the note in my fist, infuriated.

14

KAIA

I clear my throat and adjust the belt on my secondhand trench coat as I step off the elevator on the top floor of the address that Calum gave me. Stepping into a eerie white space, I look around. The room is lit from a strip of lighting that blends in with the wall; the floors are black stone. Just twenty paces away is a door that's ajar. But other than that, there are no clues for me to follow.

Definitely no sign of Calum.

My heart thrums in my chest as I move toward the doorway. The only sound is the click of my heels as I cross the dark granite floor.

Reaching the heavy door, I tug it open and step into the dimly lit space just beyond.

My eyebrows rise as I take in the huge room. The lighting in here comes from candelabras placed at strategic points against the backdrop of a huge floor to ceiling window that spans the whole space.

A stage and stripper pole are set up to the left, and a

single black leather booth. In the middle of the room there is a huge white bed, piled high with pillows. And to my right is some odd looking pleather furniture, a large wooden X, and a wall of shelves with dark boxes. I can't help but notice that one of the shelves has a bunch of sexy toys and dildos lined up on it, going from a small sleek pink device to an enormous black dildo at the end.

What in the world have I just walked into?

"Calum?" I call out. "Hello?"

A doorway opens to my left. Calum strolls out, looking like he has just walked off a runway: he's wearing a dark t-shirt and low slung jeans, his dark hair carefully messy. He sweeps his icy gaze over me, chilling me to the bone.

He smirks as he strolls toward me. "Hello, Kaia."

Goosebumps break out over my entire body. I lift my purse nervously, needing to put something between our bodies. Swallowing and lifting my chin, I lay down the law.

"I'm here." I toy with my sash. "Do you want me to just get naked?"

He arches a brow as he walks past me, to a little bar cart that's set up in the corner. "Do you want a drink?"

He pushes a button on a panel and rap music starts filtering through unseen speakers. I gulp and shake my head.

God, this whole scenario makes me so fucking nervous. My heart is fluttering like a hummingbird in my chest.

Calum waves a hand toward the bed. "Sit. I have a contract for you to sign."

He pours himself a drink as I walk over to the big bed,

perching myself on the corner. It's a little hot in here, enough to make me notice. My trench coat is over warm… but I'll be damned if I'm going to take it off until he tells me to. After all, he did say to dress to impress.

So underneath the coat I'm wearing a silky see-through black teddy, a barely there black lace bra, and the tiniest black lace thong.

Calum walks over to me, smirking, and puts down a small sheaf of paper on the bed beside me. I flush as he places a pen beside it.

He stands above me, sipping his drink and staring at me as I look at the papers.

My breath catches as I pick up the contract, skimming it. The basics I glean from reading are that he doesn't want me to tell anyone about what we're doing, he wants to be able to call me literally anytime he feels like company, and he wants me to say yes to whatever he says.

That's essentially signing away my right to say no.

I frown, looking up at him. "I don't mind most of this. But… this is basically saying that I have to say yes, no matter what you propose."

He smiles coldly. "That's right."

"What if I don't want to do something?"

He edges closer, brushing my knee with his. He looks down at me, his lips twitching.

"What do you think I want to pay you so well for? Turn the page, look at the number, and then sign the fucking contract."

My heart squeezes, my stomach flip flops. Under his cool blue gaze, it's hard to do anything but what he says.

I look at the contract, flipping to the next page. And then my heart starts beating frantically at the number I see.

A half million dollars a month.

A half a million.

Per month.

My mouth opens, but there are no words in my empty head. I glance up at him, beseeching.

And he picks up the pen, shoving it in my hands. I take it as his fingers brush my knee.

"I—"

Calum shuts me down by shaking his head. "Enough talking. Sign the contract so we can move on to other things, beauty."

His nickname for me sends chills down my spine. I uncap the pen and scrawl my name across the bottom of the page.

As I do, I'm aware that I'm making a choice.

I am selling myself to Calum.

He'll own me.

Possess me.

The ink on the dotted line begins to dry.

I toss the pen and the contract aside, shuddering as I look up into his dark eyes. He just smirks.

"Good girl."

I bite my lip and frown, not knowing what I'm supposed to say to that. Sweeping up the contract and the pen, he puts them back at the bar cart. Then he walks very slowly back to me. My heart thunders when he comes close enough that I can feel his body heat.

My head falls back and I look at him, uncertainty and

questions filling every inch of me. He looks down into my eyes with a smug expression.

"You're so beautiful," he says, reaching out his fingers to ever so lightly touch my upper arm. "So delicate. So fucking innocent. And here I am, already thinking of all the ways that I can ruin you."

My eyes widen. "Ruin me?"

He tilts his head, running his fingers across my collarbone and down into the fabric hiding my cleavage. "Oh yes, beauty. I want to make sure that no man will ever have you quite like this."

I gulp. For some reason, my eyes are drawn back to the shelf of sex toys and dildos. "Are you going to use those on me?"

My voice comes out as a soft squeak.

Calum turns his head and then gives a sharp bark of laughter when he sees what I'm looking at. "Oh, beauty. I can't wait to make you spread your legs and beg me to make you come. And those will definitely be a part of it." He swings his smoldering gaze back to me, pinning me in place. "But we should start slow. For now, I want to sit in the booth over there and watch you dance for me."

Without another word, he turns on his heel and heads left, toward the stage. I follow, closing my trench coat more tightly against my collarbone. Calum throws himself down against the black leather booth, folding his hands behind his head.

My hands shake as I grab the belt of my trench coat, walking up to him. For some reason, it's harder to take off my coat than to just be half-naked.

"Volume louder," he shouts. The music suddenly swells, shifting to a rap song I recognize.

As I untie the belt, I bite my lip and look down at the massive man that I'm about to strip for. Part of me wants to panic, to run screaming from this room.

But another part of me really wants to stay. That part of me is curious what is going to happen and doesn't care if being here is more than a little dangerous.

I take off my coat, letting it fall to the ground. Calum's eyes devour me, from my head to my toes.

"Jesus," he swears. "You are so fucking hot, Kaia."

I blush and struggle not to cover myself. "Do you want me on the pole?"

He bites his lip, smirking, and shakes his head. "No." He spreads his big hands out across his lap. "I've been waiting for you to give me another lap dance, beauty. I want to see you unravel while we are touching, just the way you almost did last time."

I raise my eyebrows, flushing hot pink. "You do?"

His lips twitch. "No more questions. Come here."

I take a step toward him before my stripper training comes back to me.

Head up. Shoulders back. Your hips should sway every time you walk.

Make him want you.

Transforming into that character is easy and natural once I remember that I should do it. I smile at him, biting my lip a little as I strut over to where he sits. His eyes sparkle as I stop just short of his reach.

"Club rules," I say, swaying my hips. "No touching, remember?"

I bend down toward him. The hint of his aftershave curls in my nose. The look on his face reminds me of a curious cat.

Calum reaches out and grabs my hips, pulling me onto his lap. "Fuck the rules. That's why I brought you here. You signed the contract. Now I can do whatever the fuck I want."

I straddle his lap, my breath leaving me in a sharp huff. "Calum…"

He lifts his hips and grinds into my ass. "Shut up."

I have to take back some semblance of control. So I clamp down on his lap and ride it for a minute, teasing him by putting my hands flat on either side of his head.

"Relax," I whisper, lifting and lowering my hips. "Let me take the reins for a minute."

I slide down a little closer to him. He shifts and his cock pops up between us, long and thick. Rocking my hips, I bump it a few times.

"Tease," he accuses. He moves again so that his cock settles against the seam of my pussy.

I rock my hips again, stopping when my movement brushes the hard tip of his cock against my clit. A very soft "Ohhh," pops out of my mouth.

It's not supposed to feel good for me, is it?

His eyes sparkle with enjoyment. "Is that the spot, beauty?"

He thrusts his hips up and his cock brushes that same spot again. My face reddens. I splay my hands out across his chest.

"I thought we were trying to get you excited," I say, a little breathlessly.

His lips twitch. He stops moving suddenly.

"You know what I want?"

I swallow, shaking my head slowly. "No."

"I want you to take off those panties and touch your clit while you ride my lap." He starts unbuttoning his jeans, his eyes glinting.

My throat works. "I—"

He moves so suddenly, ripping at my teddy and then at my panties in a frenzy. He tears my teddy in two and rips my thong off entirely, then he reaches out and pulls my bra cups down to expose my breasts.

My heart is thumping against my ribs. My eyes are open wide, my lips parted.

Is this what I signed up for? a small voice whispers in the back of my head.

"Touch yourself," he growls, looking up at me. "Show me how dirty you can be, Kaia."

He takes my hand and moves it down between us, then puts his hand in his jeans. I can only see a peek of pink flesh and he takes his cock in his fist.

Wetting my lips with my tongue, I trail my fingers down to my clit. It's swollen and needy right now, throbbing with every heartbeat. When I swipe my first two fingers over it, I almost stop breathing.

It feels good, obviously. But am I really supposed to touch myself like this with him right here? I feel his gaze on me as I circle the little nub.

What Calum is doing is far more interesting, in my opinion. He grits his teeth and works his hand up and down his shaft. I lean forward, biting my lip, trying to catch a glimpse.

His cock is enormous, not that it's any surprise. It pokes out from his jeans, dark pink and veiny, thick and uncircumcised. He catches my wide eyed look and smirks.

"Don't worry, beauty. When the time comes, you'll take the whole fucking thing in any hole I want. After I come in your mouth and take your virginity, I'm going to fuck your ass."

My jaw drops. "Calum!"

He reaches up, grabs me by the hair, and pulls my face down to his. His mouth finds my lips, plundering them mercilessly.

He pulls back for just long enough to whisper against my lips. "I'm going to come, thinking about how fucking tight your little pussy will choke my fucking cock."

My clit throbs in response, though I'm horrified. He kisses me again, more brutal this time as he jackhammers his hand up and down his cock.

He comes with a roar, sticky white semen splashing from the tip of his cock and getting all over my belly. His tongue penetrates my mouth just after he finishes, moaning as his cock twitches.

Calum releases my hair, dropping his hand and leaning back. "Fuck," he mutters. "Damn, Kaia."

My cheeks turn pink. I carefully try to extricate myself, but Calum grabs me by the back of my neck and kisses me for a long moment. His tongue works against mine, making the throb between my legs grow sharper.

Then he turns me loose. "Okay. Get up."

My face turning red, I scramble off his lap and spot my coat. Grabbing it, I pull it on and tie the belt.

Calum just lies there for another second, tucking his

cock back in his jeans. He looks at me, his mouth turning down at the corners.

"Are we done?" I blurt out, hugging myself around my waist.

His brows lower over his eyes. "Do you have somewhere else to be, Kaia?"

God, could this moment be any more mortifying?

"No," I say with a frown. "Just… if you are done, I have a long ride on the subway to get home. The sooner I leave, the sooner I can get dressed again."

He rolls his eyes and zips up his fly. "My driver will see you home."

I glare at him. "I'm fine. I'm just asking if you're… done."

He frowns. "It's not a request. And you can go. But be in the dance studio an hour early. All the really good dancers show up early to practice combinations."

My brows rise. "Oh?"

He presses a button and the music turns off. "Yes."

With that, he lumbers by me, headed back toward the door that he first entered through. I don't quite know what else to say.

But that turns out to be a good thing, because he soon disappears through the doorway, slamming the door closed behind him.

I'm left blinking at the wall where he disappeared, feeling inexplicably let down.

15

CALUM

"Ah, there he is now," Basil says.

I step through the doorway at 7:59, looking around at the dancers at their barres. Kaia is standing at the front of the right barre; she clearly took my advice to heart.

Pursing my lips, I set my water bottle down. I glance at Bas. "Are you going to begin?"

Bas shoots me a glare and then turns around, shaking his head. He raises his arms. "Okay, everyone. Let's start off in first position…"

As he continues, I prowl around the room. I'm not in a particularly good mood; I started off my morning with a conference call with some bad news about my company's stock. Now I'm here and still feeling angry.

I channel it into ballet. One of the greatest things about ballet is that you can act out your fear and anger and hatred onstage. Even greater is being a teacher and having the class make mistakes.

And this class makes a lot of mistakes. I correct every single imperfect arch and bow, remind people that their posture is essential, and always push every dancer to their god's honest limit.

Three more dancers leave in tears. Everybody else is left shaken by the end. I sit down, acting as though I need to fix my pant leg. Everyone is out of the rehearsal space like rats on a sinking ship. Even Basil hightails it out of the room.

But when the room is empty, there is still one other person. Kaia closes the door and locks it, turning to me. Putting a hand on her hip, she cocks her head.

"You're going to get yourself fired," she says levelly.

Cracking my knuckles, I push myself to my feet. "What, you can't take a little heat?"

Kaia wrinkles her nose, shaking her head. She takes a sip out of her water bottle. "If you get canned, my chances of staying in the company are slim to none."

My lips curve upward. She doesn't realize how good she is. Emma and Basil mentioned her performance during the auditions. She definitely would have been on their short list without me saying so.

But I will keep that close to my vest for now.

"I'm not going to be fired. I basically bankroll this entire place." Taking a last sip of water out of my water bottle, I cast my gaze down over Kaia's slender frame.

She's perfection today in a hot pink leotard, light pink tights, and a gauzy white dance skirt. To top it all off, there is a pink ribbon holding back her long blonde hair. That ribbon makes her look even more innocent than she is.

It makes me think of how good she's going to look wearing the same ribbon in her hair while she takes my cock deep in her throat and lets me fuck her mouth.

"Are you listening?" she asks, her brow furrowing.

One side of my mouth hitches up. "No. Are you ready to start work?"

Her hazel eyes go wide. "What?"

Stretching my arms out, I shoot her a quelling smile. "I'm supposed to tutor you," I remind her.

She blushes, but she looks relieved. "Oh. Uhhh…" She glances toward the door. "I guess now is as good a time as any. I just thought we were going to start after I had some choreography to work on."

She winces and looks down at her right foot. "Sleeping Beauty has essentially the same combinations in every iteration since the dawn of time." I nod toward her foot. "Take care of that. Then we'll start."

The door knob jiggles. I walk to the door, spying Bas through the door. Opening it, I step aside.

Basil enters, his suspicious gaze going from me to Kaia. Luckily she is already across the room, sitting on the ground and peeling off her pointe shoe.

"Why was the door locked?" Basil asks me in a hushed tone. "You can't be in a locked room with a dancer, Calum. Not with Honor, not with…" He glances at Kaia, as if trying to place her. "Whatever her name is."

I cock a brow. "I'm not sure how the door got locked. We were merely discussing her inability to arabesque from a pirouette."

He narrows his eyes on my face. "I'm warning you, Calum."

Kaia hops up, testing out her shoe. She walks over to us, looking back and forth between us. "Did you tell Bas that you're going to give me an hour of extra training twice a week?"

I smile pointedly at her. "No. We hadn't really gotten that far."

~

BASIL'S BROW WRINKLES. "Just the two of you?"

I nod. "Yep. Unless you want to stick around?"

Bas crosses his arms, looking between us. "Maybe I will. Just for today."

I want to throw him out of the room. But I don't. Instead I spread my hands wide. "Great. Kaia was just saying that she doesn't know the choreography at all yet. So maybe you can help with that."

He fixes me with a smug little glance. "Of course."

He walks over to the other side of the room, dipping his feet in the box of rosin powder to increase his traction. Then he walks to the far corner, glancing at Kaia.

"What do you want to learn first? An easy combination? Or would you prefer to start with something more advanced?"

Kaia's throat works for a second as she glances at me. "Advanced, please. I would rather do something wrong with you two here than learn easier moves."

I fold my arms across my chest and tilt my head. Bas starts out in fifth position, arching his arms upward. "Okay. So... let's start with this combination. It goes like this..."

He executes several turns and then two leaps, ending

with an arabesque. Then he does a great big leap across the floor, his movements exaggerated.

When he finishes, he looks up at Kaia. "That's one of the hardest combinations in the entirety of Sleeping Beauty. Are you ready to try it?"

She gives him a quick nod, trotting to the rosin box. After daintily dabbing her feet in the powdered tree sap, she takes her place in the far corner. She assumes fifth position, blowing out a breath.

"I can see you thinking," I call out to her. "I should see the emotion from the scene or nothing at all. You're supposed to be effortlessly graceful."

Her eyes flit to me, then refocus. Her expression turns slightly smiling. She raises her arms over her head and completes the pirouettes and the leaps. I can already see that she's too hesitant and she starts a half second too late. There is a distinctly awkward moment when she lurches out of the last turn and into the first leap.

Kaia does her big jump at the end, finishing by kicking one leg behind her and raising her arms. I blow out a breath and rub my hand over my mouth.

That performance wasn't horrible, but it was far from moving me at all.

Bas's lips twitch. "She needs music."

He pulls out his phone and plays around with the room's stereo system. I look at her with a frown.

"How did that feel for you?"

Kaia looks down, her cheeks flushing. "Not great."

"Hmm," I say, vaguely agreeing.

Lively classical music starts to play and Bas takes a deep breath. "From the top. You can turn around do the same combination going that way." He flicks his wrist to the opposite corner.

Kaia hastens to take her position. Again, I can see she's overthinking it."

"Kaia," I bark. She looks at me and I pull my hand closed in the air over my face. "Effortlessly graceful."

She nods, looking ahead and shuttering her expression. She waits for five breaths, then raises her arms and begins to step into the first turn.

This time, it's better. Her timing has improved. She clearly has a knack for pirouettes, executing them well. But the two small leaps and the grand jeté at the end fall flat.

She looks up to find me tapping my foot. "I don't understand how you made it this far through school and yet this eludes you."

Kaia shoots me a hard look. "It's only my second attempt, Calum."

Bas interrupts. "Let me see you do a turn and then step into a leap. That really needs work."

She does it again, and it looks every bit as awkward. I shake my head, moving away from the mirrored wall behind me.

"Watch," I say.

I wait a second, pulling in a breath through my nose. Then I move, turning and stepping neatly into a leap. The move requires a great deal of precision and control on my part but I execute it almost casually.

I stop short of doing another leap, turning back toward Kaia. "See?"

Her brows draw down. "I think so. I'm missing a step

between my pirouette and my leap. It's just so fast that I almost missed it."

I smirk. "Indeed."

Irritation flashes across her face for a moment before she turns and walks to the corner. She takes fifth position and begins again.

This time, her turns are close to perfect, she nails the leaps, and she manages a particularly grand jeté. She kicks her leg back behind her, balancing en pointe and raising her arms above her head.

"Hold it!" I cry. "Hold it… hold it…"

She breaks, her leg coming down. She glares at me, shaking her arms and legs out.

"Come here," I beckon. "Let's practice that arabesque."

Her gaze slides between me and Bas, who seems to be preoccupied with texting. She hurries over to stand before me, taking fifth position. Then she sweeps her leg back and up and lifts her arms.

I move closer, adjusting her posture ever so slightly with a hand on her waist. My other hand comes up to touch her inner thigh, lifting her leg ever so slightly higher.

Her eyes widen as I touch her. Her breath falters, only noticeable to me because I'm standing so close.

It is very tempting to slide my hand down to tease her pussy and up to nudge her breast. But I don't.

Even if I were to give in, Bas is standing right behind us. He's waiting for just that kind of move from me.

So I stay put. I can feel Kaia's muscles start to tremble under my fingers.

In this moment, she is graceful and beautiful.

"One more…" I whisper.

She holds it for another half breath before slowly releasing. I step back, putting my hands behind my back.

"That was good," I say.

Kaia looks at me, her wide hazel eyes taking me in. Her cheeks turn pink and she tucks a stray lock of her hair that has escaped her ribbon back behind her ear.

"Don't think so much," I murmur. "The pose is not easy, but it should be calming for you. After so much motion it is your reward. Just being still for a few moments."

Bas smiles lightly, looking at his phone. "I should go. Good work today though, Kaia."

Kaia blushes and ducks her head. "Have a good night."

Bas purses his lips and arches a brow at me while he walks out of the studio. I'm not sure what that was exactly, but I'm sure that he wouldn't leave me here with Kaia if he knew what kind of thoughts I've had about her in the last twenty four hours.

As he leaves, I heave a sigh. "Do you want to run it again? Repetition builds muscle memory."

She puffs out her cheeks and puts her hands on her hips, nodding as she walks across the room. "Yeah."

We drill the same combination about ten more times. "Good. Again."

As I walk over and check my phone, I see twenty missed calls, from Lucas and from another number that I don't recognize. As I'm scrolling through my texts from Lucas, I see this.

Anita had a bad fall. They are taking her to Memorial

Hospital with a suspected fractured hip and a possible concussion. Call me.

And then, *where the fuck are you, Calum?*

"Fuck," I say, glowering at my phone.

"What?" Kaia calls.

"Nothing. Don't worry about it. I have to go," I say, not even looking at her.

I have to take control of this situation or Anita is going to have Lucas eating out of the palm of her hand soon enough. Not even glancing back, I grab my water bottle and start calling my limousine driver.

CALUM

I ride the elevator upstairs to the twelfth floor of Memorial Hospital, brooding as the floors tick by. The doors open to reveal a white block that serves as a desk and runs to my right and to my left.

I step out and stalk to the desk, looking over the nurses who are doing paperwork. "1217?"

One of the nurses looks at me, her eyes narrowing. "Are you family?"

My lips curl up in a sneer. I'm certainly not a blood relative, but Lucas and I are all that Anita has. She's driven away everyone else.

"She wants to see me," I say. I can see the door on the right side of the hall, labeled 1201. Starting toward it, I flap a hand at the nurse. "I got it."

"Sir?" Another nurse calls after me. "Sir, you need to check in—"

Picking up the pace, I turn the corner and walk down the eerily quiet hall. Everything but the doors is white; the doors are antiseptic seafood green, most closed for privacy.

Here and there, placed at staggered intervals, are odd numbered doors.

1213… 1215… 1217.

I find the door, turning and facing it. The same nurse has followed me down the hall, her expression uncertain.

I realize my heart is thumping in my chest as I suck in a deep breath. Before I can make a move to open the door, it swings open wide. I see my brother's dark hair first as he turns from saying something to the room's occupant.

"I'll get—" Lucas sees me and his eyebrows rise. "You're here."

I squint at him. "I am," I agree. "You said it was an emergency."

He moves forward, closing the door behind himself and puffing out his cheeks. "Yeah." He checks the hallway, waving to the nurse. "Hey, can you call Dr. Stein? She is complaining that the pain medication is making her nauseated. We need to try another one."

The nurse slows, looking between us. It takes too long for Lucas, who pulls out his phone. "I'm going to call the head of medicine. What's your name again? I want to make sure I get it right."

She swallows. "Sandra! I'm Sandra. And… no need to call Dr. Baker again. I'll call Dr. Stein right now."

She hurries away, her thick soled shoes squeaking on the floor. I arch a brow.

"How many times have you called Dr. Baker already?"

He shrugs a shoulder. "For what we pay in charitable donations, I'll call Dr. Baker every ten minutes until Anita is out of the hospital."

I take a deep breath. "What happened?"

"She said she fell getting out of the shower." He screws up his face. "She hit her head pretty hard and bruised her left hip."

I narrow my eyes at him, calculating. "Are you saying that you brought me all the way across Manhattan in rush hour traffic because Anita has a bruise?"

He rolls his eyes dismissively. "She asked for you."

"Uh huh." I fold my arms across my chest. "Where is Manuelo?"

Lucas heaves a sigh and sticks his hands in the pockets of his dark slacks. "She wouldn't say. It seems like they had a spat, I guess. She kept saying that he's been gone for a while."

My upper lip curls. "Manuelo works for us, Lucas. Why didn't you just call him?"

He pushes his cheek out with his tongue. "Don't take your distemper out on me, Calum. I tried his number; it has been disconnected. So Anita was my only source and she was less than forthcoming…"

"Lucas?"

Her voice comes faintly through the door. The sound of her nasal tone sends a wave of nausea through my whole system. It also causes me to break into a cold sweat.

Lucas turns around and pushes the door open. "Look who is here, Anita."

He grabs me by the forearm and tows me into the room. Anita is sitting on the hospital bed, her tiny body surrounded by pillows and smothered in blankets. She sits up a little and pats the back of her dyed black hair, her mouth pursing. Whether she is displeased or not is impossible to say.

"Oh, Calum," she says, tearing up. She speaks English heavily inflected with a Spanish accent. "Thank god you're here. I keep telling everybody to wait until you get here to make my medical decisions."

My mouth thins. "I'm not interested in having any say in what happens to you, Anita. I think I've made that clear as a bell."

Lucas gives me an alarmed look, but I'm not worried about that. Anita does exactly what I expect of her, which is that she bursts into full-fledged tears.

"Why do you treat me as if I was some street trash, Cal? After I raised you, after I fed and clothed and sheltered you out of my own pocket?!"

She starts sobbing brokenly. I check my watch; it took her less than two minutes to start guilt tripping me about having basic needs as a child.

Lucas shoves me. I roll my eyes up at him, scowling. "What?"

"Be nice to her," he mutters. "Jesus, Calum. She's in the fucking hospital."

I glare at him. He glares right back.

"You shouldn't have called me here," I say simply. "You know better."

The nurse coughs gently behind us to alert us to her presence. "Excuse me, but could I please borrow you, Mr. Fordham?"

Lucas stiffens. "Yeah, of course. Coming."

I scowl at him as he leaves the room, stalking down the hallway. Anita has progressed to full blown howling by now; I blow out a breath as I cast a glance her way.

"You treat me so terrible!" she wails.

I lean against the closest wall, tilting my head. "What happened to Manuelo, Anita? Hmm? Lucas said that he changed his phone number."

Her thin shoulders shake with the force of her sobs. "Se ha ido! Como tu. Ya no es especial para mi!!"

"Yeah, I still don't speak any Spanish." I glance behind me, wondering when Lucas is coming back.

She cries for a minute. When she yells again, it's accentuated with hiccups. "I. Don't. Know. Why. You. Don't. CARE about me!"

"Yes, you do." I look at my fingernails, pursing my lips.

"No!" she shrieks.

"Well, the second my mother died, you offered to take care of me and Lucas." My lips twitch. "And before she was even buried, you came onto me. I was fifteen. My mom had just died." I smile at her, the expression turning mean. "And if I'm remembering correctly, you made me fuck you in a closet at her funeral."

"What!?" she cries. "No, you were older than that when we made love! You said you were in love with me, *mijo*."

I exhale a long breath. "No, I didn't. And I wasn't. Should we call a few of the nurses in here and ask them if they think that was an okay thing to do to a boy who's mom had just died?" I narrow my eyes. "Or how about I finally tell Lucas that the whole time we were with you, the whole time we were enrolled in ballet school and living a life of luxury… you were fucking me every single chance you got. Hmm?"

She suddenly stops crying, her sniffles making her

sound even more pathetic. "I don't think other people can understand, mi amor. What we had was a soul connection."

Anita grips the blankets, pulling them closer.

I snort. "Whatever you have to tell yourself, Anita. Just remember that I can tell everyone that little bit of gossip anytime I feel like it."

She sniffs, wiping at her nose. "You're hateful. You always have been. Ever since you were little, you always would cause a problem."

"Let me ask you something. How old was I when you first looked at me and thought, I want to fuck him. Fourteen? Thirteen?"

She glares at me. "You were born like this, mijo. You were born ruined like trash in the summertime."

Her words don't even prick me. I just laugh. "So younger than thirteen, then. That's disgusting."

"You are a pig of a man," she fires back.

I put my hands to my heart, playing as if she'd wounded me. "Tough words, coming from a pedophile."

I'm not sure how she even reached over and flung her water bottle at me so fast, but it sprays the entire lower half of the wall near me. I look down at the few drips of moisture that hit my shins.

"Is that all you've got?" I goad her. Laughing, I point a finger at her. "Take me off your contact list. I don't want to be called back here for you."

Lucas pops his head back in the room. He takes a breath, sensing the tension in the air between us. Anita is glaring at me; I still wear a half smile.

"O…kay. Calum, can I talk to you for a minute out here?"

I shoot Anita one last cold smile. "Gladly."

Walking out of her room is heavenly. Closing the door on her sniveling face is just the cherry on top of my fucking sundae. I turn to my brother, squinting.

"If you're about to ask me a favor, the answer is no," I tell him. "I'm not helping you help her."

He takes a step toward me, his face twisting into a sneer, and pushes me so that my back hits the wall. "What the hell is your problem, Calum? Can't you have a little compassion? That woman in there was basically our second mother."

That sick feeling washes through my stomach once again. "Don't say that, Lucas. I know our mom had her problems—"

He pushes me again. "Mom was a drug addict. Okay? And a prostitute. And Anita stepped in, though she didn't have to, and took really good care of us. She spent like a hundred thousand dollars to make sure we were accepted at the best ballet school and we would both go on to have our own careers in ballet. And she's nice, on top of all that."

My lips twist in a grimace. "There are things you don't know," I warn.

He shakes his head in disbelief. "Tell me! If she really did something that terrible and I somehow missed it, tell me right now! Come on, we'll go to the police together, since it is obviously a terrible crime that must be punished…"

I glare at him. My hands ball into fists. As much as I want to tell him, want to rub it in his smug face, I won't.

I can't tell him that I slept with Anita to keep a roof

over our heads and food in our mouths. Part of me is too proud and another part of me just… doesn't want him to live with that kind of guilt.

So I stonewall him. "It's none of your business."

He laughs. "That's what I fucking thought."

I lean in close to his face. "You don't know her like I do, Lucas."

"Can you stop? I'm sorry, okay? I'm sorry I called you to come help me handle this situation."

That gives me pause. I would do anything for Lucas. He's the one person in the world that I would walk through fire and crawl on my belly over shards of glass to help.

I compose myself, shutting down the emotions I'm feeling. "Just tell me what you need, Lucas."

He blows out a breath, taking a step back. He tilts his head to the side. "All I need is the names and phone numbers of some replacements for Manuelo. And maybe some second opinions, just to check Anita out and make sure that she's really okay."

My lips twitch. He could've asked one of our personal assistants for those numbers. But I won't get into that right now.

"Fine."

He narrows his eyes on my face. "Fine."

I repress an eye roll. "I'm going to go. I'll have Jane reach out to you within the next hour."

He purses his lips. "Okay."

I turn and stride down the hall. He calls, "Thanks!"

Without looking back, I wave a dismissive hand, heaving a silent sigh.

17

KAIA

I'm busy tonight.

I glance at my cellphone again, wondering what that text from Calum means. What is he doing?

Shopping for yachts? Visiting his tailor to buy another dozen custom made suits? Eating sushi with models? The last idea tugs the corners of my mouth downward.

"Hey!" Ella says, reaching out and jerking me to the right.

I look up and realize that I almost walked into a huge potted plant placed in the middle of the walkway down to the bowling alley. Screwing my face up, I sigh and put my phone in the back pocket of my jeans. "Thanks."

Ella shakes her head at me, running a hand over her short baby blue dress. "You have been glued to your phone ever since I picked you up. What's so important?"

I wrinkle my nose. "Nothing."

She holds my arm as she tows me inside the bowling alley. Just beyond the doors there is the desk with an irritated person mousing through a computer. Just beyond that is a towering stack of cubbies, each jammed full of shoes. Even if I was blind, I could tell where we are; the pungent smell of disinfectant rises to my nose and the immediate blast of air conditioning on my skin see to that.

The clerk looks up at us, squinting a little. "You wanna bowl or what?"

Ella steps forward, pursing her lips. "Yeah. We are joining someone…"

Looking out across the brightly colored lanes, I spot Eric. I nudge Ella and she clears her throat. "Lane four. We need…" She looks at me, lifting her brows. "What, an hour?"

The guy sighs. "Two people, two pairs of shoes, one hour. That's fifteen bucks."

Before Ella can get her wallet out of her purse, I fish a twenty dollar bill out of my pocket. "Here."

The clerk doesn't even look at me. He just hands me change and hurries to get us each a pair of shoes. Then we walk over to where Eric is lounging, his feet up on the small screen where you input names.

"Hey," Ella says.

He salutes both of us lazily. "You were supposed to be here twenty minutes ago."

"Sorry," I instantly apologize. "Ella was on time. I was running behind as usual."

He smirks a little at me, his gaze traveling down my body. "It's nice to see that you have a t-shirt and jeans. I was starting to think that all you owned were leotards and leg warmers."

I flush at his teasing. Ella plops herself down in a nearby seat, changing her shoes. I do the same, my eyes traveling up to where Eric has already filled in nicknames for each of us.

"I know I'm Kaia Papaya," I say, putting my other shoes under a seat. "But who are the other two names?"

He stands up, stretching. "I'm E-Male. Get it, cause I'm the only guy?"

"Does that make me Old Yella?" Ella asks. "I do not get your sense of humor, my dude."

Eric rolls his eyes. "Can we just bowl?"

I take a deep breath and nod. "Let me pick out a ball really quickly."

His lips twitch. "I already put a couple of twelve pound balls in the ball return thing."

I arch my eyebrows. "For me?"

He squints at me. "For both of you. The last time we did this, you both used twelve pound balls. Since I had nothing but time while I was waiting on you, I went ahead and grabbed four balls that size. Plus a sixteen pounder for myself."

I blink. "Oh. Well… thanks. That was really nice of you."

Ella points up at the scoreboard. "According to that, you're up first, Eric."

He stands up, brushing imaginary dust off of his dark t-shirt. "Watch and learn, ladies."

I smile, rolling my eyes. Ella wrinkles her nose.

"In your dreams, white boy," she calls after him. "I'm going to whoop you."

As I watch him select his ball, I reach into my back pocket for my phone. I check the screen but there are no notifications.

Heaving a silent sigh, I return the phone to my jeans. Ella arches a questioning eyebrow at me. "Who is keeping you from being present right now?"

I flush. "No one. I'm just… checking my Insta."

The lie sounds phony coming out of my mouth. "You are a terrible liar." Crossing her arms, she turns to watch Eric bowl.

I bite my lip and do the same. Eric knocks some pins down, trotting back towards us.

"Just getting warmed up," he says, bridging his hands and turning them inside out. "I'm telling you guys, I'm a great bowler."

I giggle. "We have bowled with you before. There is no reason to lie."

"Yeah, E-Male," Ella says, laughing.

Eric's face flushes. "You can both go to hell."

"Hmm." Ella shakes her head and looks at the scoreboard. "Hey, I'm going to grab one of every kind of junk food from the commissary. Any special requests?"

I turn and look at the restaurant, if you can call a popcorn machine and one of those hot dog rollers that. Wrinkling my nose, I pull out some cash. "Get me whatever is the best bang for my buck."

She eyes me. "Look at you, Miss Got Money To Burn All The Sudden. Keep your dough. This is my treat. Just be prepared to eat your own weight in salty, sticky, sweet goodness."

She wiggles her eyebrows and dashes off toward the food counter. Her dress barely covers her ass as she goes but I figure she already knows all about that.

"Your turn," Eric says quietly. He's close behind me and that gives me a start.

I whirl around, my eyes wide. "What?"

He points up at the scoreboard, where Kaia Papaya is flashing insistently. "It's your turn to bowl."

I give him a wobbly smile. "Right. Duh."

I walk past him. He leans into my path, bumping my shoulder with his. I scrunch my nose up and shoot him a joking glare.

"Watch it!" I protest.

He smirks at me as he sits down. In his blue jeans and snug t-shirt, with his light blue eyes and sandy blond hair, he looks like the all-American boy. The football player who you hope will ask you to homecoming.

I flush as I grab the closest ball from the ball return. In any other scenario, I would be over the moon that someone as handsome as Eric was flirting with me.

In fact, deep down, I have butterflies rumbling around in my stomach.

But as I walk toward the bowling lane, I can't be truly happy about it. Because there is one tall, dark, and irresistibly smug problem.

Calum. Add the money he pays me and the fact that I've fooled around with him more than anybody else…

And yeah. Eric is dreamy. But Calum is…

Well, he's a man. With dark three piece suits, a tumbler of whiskey, and stunning ocean blue eyes, I might add.

So what if we don't really have anything more than a transactional relationship? Maybe it's better that way.

We have rules. We have boundaries.

No one will get hurt.

"Can you throw the ball already?" Eric asks.

"Don't rush me!" I say.

I wind up and toss the ball, biting my lip. As it sails neatly down the middle of the lane, I shrug. The ball strikes the pins; all the pins go down, just as I intended.

"Yes!" I cheer. I turn around, doing a little victory dance. Striding back from the lane, I grin at Eric. "That was a strike, in case you missed it."

Eric rolls his eyes. "Yeah, yeah. I just have to get loose and then we'll see who's good at this game."

Just in time for her turn, Ella comes walking down from the restaurant, her arms loaded with all kinds of food. "A little help?"

I trot over to the closest table, helping relieve her burden. She wasn't wrong about getting one of every-thing. She sets down chicken fingers, curly fries, two orders of cheese sticks, and several long, sweet smelling churros. She also plunks down a pitcher of soda and cups.

"One more thing…" she says. Then she reaches in her little purse and tosses a pack of Sour Patch Kids on the table.

I look at all the food, my eyes widening. "This is a lot. Do you know how many calories are on this table right now?"

Ella narrows her eyes at me. "I got you diet soda, okay? So let's all just enjoy the bounty."

I smile at her. "Thanks."

"Holy shit," Eric says, coming up to the table. "I volunteer to be your personal Hoover, vacuuming up anything that's leftover."

She grins. "Help yourself. I'm going to go bowl this frame right quick."

Eric rubs his hands together, snagging a seat. I sit down opposite him, pouring out the diet soda first. He chooses to bite in a churro first, moaning.

"Oh man," he whispers, almost reverent. "It's been a while since I had something that was deep fried."

I smirk, opening my pack of candy. "Yeah?"

Ella returns after a minute, grabbing a cheese stick and enthusiastically dipping it in a little plastic ramekin of marinara. "God, I might have fantasized about this a little bit on the way over here." She takes a bite and then groans. "This is the best thing I've ever eaten. I'm not even lying."

Shaking my head, I grab a curly fry and bite into it. It's a little overcooked but still hot.

"Okay, these fries are amazing and someone will have to take them away from me at some point."

My phone buzzes in my pocket.

I chew my fry and try to sneak it out of my pocket, checking the screen under the table. Of course it's nothing, just a stupid email notification. Ella leans over to see and then rolls her eyes.

"Seriously?"

My cheeks turn bright pink. "What? My phone buzzed!"

She shakes her head, turning to Eric. "She has checked her phone no less than twenty times in the last hour. That tells me that she's waiting to hear from some hot ass booty call—"

"Ella!" I cry, embarrassed. "I'm telling you, I'm just... like, a phone addict or whatever."

Eric looks at me, his expression cautious. "Who are you expecting to hear from? We are your only friends… and we are here."

I point at them both. "That's not true. I have other, non-ballet friends."

Ella laughs. "You do not. It's okay, I don't have friends outside of ballet either. I mean, there are my cousins. I hang out with them a lot when I'm at home, but that's just because my family has the nicest house."

She rolls her eyes.

Eric nods at my phone. "Who are you waiting to hear from, Kaia?"

I will do just about anything to avoid that question. So I smile, turning to Ella.

"Hey, remember last year when Eric was dancing, doing all the Russian jumps, and his pants pretty much exploded?"

He glares at me, swiping a chicken finger. "I'm sure everyone has moved on from that."

Ella snorts. "Uh, noooo. We didn't forget. That was the day that I found out that you wear a dainty pink dance belt under your leggings."

He rocks his head back. "I washed the damn belt with a red shirt. It turned pink in the wash. I thought I already explained that!"

Before the argument can continue, my phone starts buzzing in my hand. Alarmed, I look down at the screen.

Calum.

My heart starts to beat wildly. My stomach fills with acid.

"Umm, I should go take this," I mumble, sliding to my feet.

"I told you there was a boy," Ella said. "Didn't I tell you?"

Hurrying away from the table, I put the phone to my ear. "Hello?"

There is no greeting, no warm tone. Just his gruff rumble. "I need you dressed in cocktail attire and ready to meet me at Peychaud's in an hour."

"Uhhh…" I glance back at my friends. "I'm really in the middle of something. Besides, I'm not dressed right…"

"I'm texting you the address now," he says. "Don't make me wait."

Then he hangs up, leaving me staring at my home screen. I blink several time, then turn toward my friends, trying to decide just what I'm about to tell them to escape.

18

CALUM

I'm at the stylish, hammered copper bar at Peychaud's, toying with my drink. The lights are dimmed, the place is hopping. It's busy tonight, the bar packed, the tables full of noisy people dressed in their date night best.

The bartender, a pretty brunette, comes over to check on me. "Would you like another Vieux Carre?"

I look down at the drink, surprised to find it all but empty. The dark cherry is still there along with a couple of half-melted cubes of ice. I check my watch with a sigh.

"Yeah. Might as well."

She takes my old glass and heads down the bar. Right beside me, a group of young businesspeople throw their heads back, laughing hysterically. A redhead in a stunning red dress accidentally steps too far back. She whirls, her expression a bit tipsy but no less apologetic.

"Omigoooooddd," she squeaks. "I'm so sorry."

I frown at her. Normally I would use this moment to

pick her up and fuck her in a storage closet. But Kaia is on her way here.

At least, in theory.

I've gone to great lengths to have Kaia at my beck and call; I know for a fact that she'll give me exactly what I'm looking for, because I pay her to.

Which is why the redhead is off-limits, for now.

"No problem," I say at last, starting to turn away.

She leans closer, peering at me with an incredulous look on her face. "Your eyes are stunning!" She says. "You're not here all by yourself, are you?"

I glance at my watch again. Kaia is twenty minutes late. Which begs the question…

Am I here alone or not?

Before I can answer her, I notice Kaia outside the window, dressed in a tiny white dress. She's running toward the bar, looking flustered.

"My date just got here," I say. "You'll excuse me…"

I turn and signal to the bartender to keep my seat and the chair beside it open. Then I walk over to the front door, where Kaia is being hassled by the door guy for ID.

I pull out my money clip and slide off a hundred dollar bill, waving it at the guy. "She's with me."

He doesn't even blink or look up at me. He just takes the money and turns to the next person coming through the door.

Kaia looks at me, trying to catch her breath. She looks absolutely amazing, her tits pushed up and an almost scandalous amount of leg showing. I step closer, hugging her against my dark-suited body.

My lips twitch as I whisper in her ear. "You're late."

She pulls back, her eyes scanning my face. "I told you. I was on the other side of town."

Guiding her back to our seats at the bar, I pull her seat out for her. Her eyebrows rise.

"Are you being a gentleman for me now, Calum?"

I chuckle as I take my own seat. "Don't worry, beauty. I promise that I'm still beastly underneath this posh exterior. I'm Dr. Jekyll right now, but wait until I get you alone."

I smile at her, showing my teeth. She shivers as her eyes dip down to my mouth. I can't get enough of those honest, innocent little reactions.

She licks her lips nervously, looking over at the bar. She leans close, whispering to me. "I'm not actually old enough to be in here."

I squint at her. Yes, I know that I should pick women who are old enough to legally drink. And I usually do.

But Kaia is different. One look at her body while she was grinding on the pole at Club X and I knew I had to have her.

"Here," I say, picking up the Vieux Carre cocktail. "Try this."

She takes a sip, looking at me. Then she makes a face. "It's strong. And bitter. I… I don't think I like it, Calum."

I roll my eyes. "All right. We'll start off easy. You like champagne, right?"

Her cheeks blaze bright pink. "Yes…"

I raise my hand as a signal. The bartender comes over, smiling. "What can I make for you?"

"Make her a French 75," I say.

The bartender nods, disappearing. When she reappears

a half minute later, she holds a champagne flute. The contents of the glass are a curl of lemon, a little gin, a dash of simple syrup, and an effervescent champagne topper.

"Here you go," she says, setting it on a cocktail napkin before Kaia. "Enjoy."

"Thanks," Kaia says. She looks at me again as she tastes the cocktail. As though she needs feedback from me when sampling something new.

That's… *interesting*.

Her expression brightens. "Mmm! This is good."

I smile coolly. "Baby's first cocktail."

"Hmm?" she asks, leaning her head closer to my mouth.

"Never mind. Where were you when I called?"

Her mouth pulls down in a frown. "Here and there. Out with my friends."

I narrow my eyes on her face. "What friends?"

I move my hand toward her cheek, thinking to tuck a piece of her cornsilk hair back behind her ear. But I'm not expecting her reaction.

Kaia flinches, closing her eyes and recoiling. I stop, my hand hovering in the air between us.

It's the first time I've seen her behave like that, as if she were an abused puppy and I were her unhinged owner.

That's a learned behavior if I've ever seen one.

After a second, she opens her eyes. Warmth instantly rushes to her cheeks.

"Sorry," she says, looking mortified. "You… uh…"

I shrug one shoulder, dropping my hand. Instead I pick up my drink, taking a sip. The cool liquid burns on its way down.

Kaia puts her champagne flute on the bar, pouting. "Is it usually like this? When you… start seeing someone like me? Or am I just spectacularly awkward?"

"I wouldn't know," I say.

She looks up at me, surprised. "What do you mean?"

"You're not the first girl to catch my eye at Club X," I say, swirling the amber contents around in my tumbler. "But you are definitely the first one that I've seen outside the club. The only one I've had a contract with."

She blinks, flushing. "Oh. I just assumed that you had… *dated*… women from the club before."

I purse my lips and cock my head. "You caught my eye. But you had my attention the second that I saw you do an arabesque. The stripping was all flash, but the actual ballet is the reason that we are both here right now."

I reach out, trailing my fingers over her knee. She looks up, swallowing hard, her hazel eyes so wide and innocent.

"Don't you agree?" I murmur.

She sinks her white teeth into the fullness of her bottom lip, smiling shyly. "I never quite know what to think when I'm around you."

I smirk at her. "I promise to keep you on your toes… quite literally."

She squints at me. "Did you just make a pun?"

I shrug, glancing away and sipping my drink. "I can be funny sometimes. Mostly when I am drunk."

She nods slowly. "It's just not something I associate with you as a person."

"What can I say, I'm multifaceted. You didn't think

that you could know me for less than a month and already have me all figured out, did you?"

Two spots of pink appear in the apples of her cheeks. She wrinkles her nose humorously. "I guess not. But… does your comedic turn mean you are drunk right now?"

Setting my drink on the bar, I move toward her, skimming my hands along the outside of her bare thighs. "I'm getting there. Don't worry, beauty. My dick is still hard as a fucking rock right now, looking at you in that little dress."

She bites her lip playfully, placing her hand on my shoulder to pull my ear closer to her mouth. "I've been thinking about you a lot. Thinking about when I straddled your lap and you rubbed my pussy…"

Growling softly, I stand up and pull her hard against the wall of my muscular body. She makes a soft sound of surprise, looking up at me. She's so soft, so feminine. So innocent, a rose whose petals are ready to be plucked.

I bite my lip, whispering in her ear. "I'm going to ruin you, Kaia. After we finally fuck, no other man will ever make you cream the same way."

She looks at me, sucking in a breath. I reach up and drag my thumb across the fullness of her sensitive bottom lip. She leans her head back a little, her lips parting, her eyes closing halfway.

I can't help but kiss her, pressing my lips against her hot mouth. Her fingers curl around my nape; she moans ever so softly as I sweep the inside of her mouth with my tongue.

She's so fucking sweet that I almost can't stand it. I

groan and press her closer, my hand sliding down from her waist to cup her ass.

My cock throbs, pressed between our bodies. A stray image pops into my head of her on her knees, her mouth open wide as I bury my cock deep and fuck her face. The feeling of her tongue working against mine makes my whole body shudder.

I pull back, ready to tell her that we should go to my limo. But over her shoulder, I see Honor standing with her hands on her hips. She's wearing a little silver dress and showing off a lot of skin. It would be hotter if I didn't know that she was out at a bar while she was pregnant. She looks at both of us, her lips twisting sourly.

"Am I seeing things?" she asks. "Because if I'm not mistaken, this is one of the dancers that the New York Ballet brought in to replace me."

Kaia's eyes widen and she steps away from me, glancing back at Honor. "Says who?"

"Don't engage with your predecessor, Kaia. She's clearly been trolling the NYB's website, angry at being replaced." I tilt my head to the side. "How is being pregnant going for you, Honor?"

She scoffs. "Like you can judge me. I know that you two are not supposed to be all over each other like this. I mean, you're supposed to be her teacher, Calum. Jesus."

I shoot her a glare. "We should go, Kaia."

Honor blocks our path. "Seriously? The last time I checked, you were obsessed with me. I practically had to take a restraining order on your fucking ass. What happened?"

I slide my arm around Kaia's waist, tugging her close

as I start to maneuver around Honor. "You had plenty of chances, Honor. Clearly I've found a replacement for you."

Kaia does a double take. "What?"

Honor bares her teeth. "I want my job back, Calum."

I shake my head, pulling Kaia along with me. "I don't really care."

"I'll report you both!" Honor calls after us.

I stop, releasing Kaia from my grip. Turning around slowly, I send Honor a smoldering glare. "You're an aging, bitter, disgraced former employee. I don't think that anyone will listen to you make accusations against me, the primary supporter of the ballet company." I smirk. "So go right ahead. I would love to get you on record so that my fleet of personal attorneys can destroy you."

Honor's eyes widen. "Calum—"

I shake my head, spinning back to Kaia. "Let's go."

Kaia lets me pull her along, glancing back as we leave the bar. We step outside and my limousine is already waiting. I get the door, pulling it open for her.

But she doesn't get in. Her eyebrows are drawn down, her mouth is twisted to the side. "Is what you said true? Am I really just a replacement for Honor?"

That gives me pause. "No. I don't… it's more complicated than that. Can you get in the fucking car?"

She balks. "I think I can get my own ride tonight."

"Seriously?!" I protest. "Get in the fucking limo, Kaia. If you insist, I can drop you off at your house."

Kaia stares at me, her hands bunching into fists. "Fine," she says through clenched teeth. She ducks her head and climbs in the back seat.

I get in after her, pissed off. Honor managed to ruin a perfectly good mood. And now I'm chauffeuring Kaia home instead of having her enthusiastically blow me.

"Where are we going?" I ask, bristling.

Kaia looks away, out the limo's window. "Queens."

The limousine pulls out and I glare at the buildings as they pass, seething.

19

KAIA

"She said that you are the biggest backstabber that she's ever met," the bleach blonde housewife says. From my computer screen, she squints at the woman she's dishing gossip to. Because she's had so much plastic surgery done to her face, she looks almost serene even though her voice is angry.

I am sitting in full splits on the floor of my living area, watching tv on my ancient laptop. My apartment doesn't have any heat of its own. Instead I rely on ambient heat from the tenants below, several tiny space heaters, and a ton of blankets and socks.

Still, my apartment is chilly today. The people downstairs must have their heat turned down during the day. I wrap myself up in my prized possession, my dove gray winter coat.

It is heavy and warm and made of wool. I brought it at a thrift store for pennies on the dollar and I unabashedly love it.

As the women on my screen escalate tensions, I lower

my upper body onto the floor. My kitty Exupéry swishes his tail, disapproving of my focusing on anything that isn't him.

I raise myself onto my elbows with a sigh and pet him. "I know. You don't like Kelly either, huh? Who could?"

The cat meows are rubs against my hand. I feel sort of bad for Exupéry because I am almost never home. But there is a kitty door downstairs that Exupéry seems to make full use of whenever I'm not around.

"You probably have like eight other families," I say, scratching her chin. "I get it. I'm just not around very much, am I? I wouldn't even be here right now, except that Basil is sick. So I get a full day off."

She cocks her head and looks at me, giving me one last rub before strutting off. I sigh and think about food; I can't remember the last time that I went grocery shopping.

I sit up and pull my laptop in, pursing my lips. Maybe I need to go shopping at like… a farmer's market. That sounds healthy… and way cheaper and closer than some place like Whole Foods.

I type in farmer's market in my search bar and a million results pop up. I scroll through the results, not seeing exactly what I'm looking for.

There is a sudden knock at my door, a loud enough banging that I tense and shut my laptop. This is definitely out of the ordinary because no one knows where I live.

Well, except Calum.

Why would he not call me first, though?

I scramble to stand, brushing off my jeans and lilac midriff tee. The knocking comes again, sounding even more aggressive this time.

"Coming!" I call, trotting to the stairs and thundering down them. The banging persists even as I wrench open the door.

"Okay, okay—"

I stop mid sentence, blinking.

My father stands there in his slacks and a dark fleece jacket, looking angry. A few steps down, Hazel stands with her hands in the pockets of her stylish black silk jumpsuit.

"Oh. Hi?" I say, squinting at both of them.

My dad smiles, showing his teeth. "Your sister and I were just in the city, meeting with some people for her fashion label. We thought we should just stop by."

I narrow my eyes at them both. It's the first time I've heard about my sister having a fashion label, but I let that pass.

"How did you know to find me here?" I ask, glancing out the door. "And why didn't you call?"

My father's smile broadens. "Can't you just be happy to see your family, Kaia?"

I flick my gaze to Hazel, who is smiling smugly. "Of course. I mean… do you guys want to come in?"

My heart starts racing. I definitely don't want either of them in my private space, my innermost sanctum. For a second, my breath hitches as my father looks past me, considering.

When he shakes his head, I'm beyond relieved.

"I thought we would all get some lunch. Some-where…" He glances around him, his lips twitching. He obviously doesn't like my neighborhood very much. "Nice."

I suck in a deep breath. "Yeah, sure. Let me just grab my shoes and my purse."

I turn around and clatter up the stairs, quickly finding them. My dad and my sister have a cab waiting when I come back down; only fifteen minutes later, we are back in Manhattan proper.

"Where are we going?" I ask.

My dad glances back at me from the passenger seat. "We're almost there."

I glance at Hazel, who is playing on her phone. "How is school?"

She rolls her eyes over to me. "You don't need to act interested in my life, Kaia. I have plenty of my own friends and interests."

My eyebrows rise. "Okay… I was just checking in."

The car stops before she has time to retort. My father jumps out, opening the door for Hazel. He offers her his arm as I climb out of the other side, looking at the restaurant we are going into.

"Adolpho's," I read out loud. It looks fancy, with gold-plated doors and a Sicilian flag displayed out front.

"Hurry up, Kaia," Dad says. "We don't want to be late."

I scrunch up my face as I scurry after them. My father pushes through the gold-plated door. As I follow him into the lush, dim interior, I'm greeted with the rather heavenly smells of pasta and red sauce.

My stomach audibly rumbles.

My father and Hazel walk right by the host, so I just follow them into the swanky dining room. There are a few tables of people sitting at black leather booths. My dad makes a beeline for what is obviously the nicest seat in the place, a big corner booth with someone already sitting in it.

I scrutinize the older man who is sitting there. Salt and pepper hair, on the short side, thin as a rail.

He looks up as my father slides into the booth across from him, his lips twisting. "Don, I thought you were going to be a no-show."

My father smiles broadly, scooting over to make room for Hazel and me. "Sorry about that. Traffic here in the city is just the pits."

My brows rise. It might be the first time I've ever heard my dad apologize; whoever this guy is, he definitely has more money or power than my dad does.

My dad waves at my sister and me as we sit down. "These are my daughters, Hazel and Kaia. Kaia is the one I was telling you about, Tony. The little ballerina."

Tony's shrewd gaze falls on me. He tilts his head, his gaze calculating.

"Nice to meet you. Tony Cardezzio. I'm a business associate of your father's."

He doesn't move to offer his hand, so I just bob my head. "Nice to meet you, sir."

Hazel just smirks quietly, saying nothing. Tony clears his throat, looking at my father. I start getting a weird vibe; everybody at this table is acting really strangely.

I frown at the rest of the table but I don't say anything. A waiter rushes up, his notepad at the ready.

"Can I get you anything to drink?" he asks.

Tony purses his lip. "I'll tell you what. Get me and my friend here each a glass of red wine. We'll both have a steak, medium well done, with a baked potato. These two ladies will have salads, dressing on the side."

I blink. Unease slides through my stomach as the waiter nods and vanishes toward the kitchen. I am not sure why this stranger just ordered my food.

I would gladly rather order for myself and pay for my own food. I'm sure that mostly people would feel the same. But looking at my father, I can't figure out why he doesn't say a single word.

"So, Kaia," Tony says, steeling his fingers. "You do ballet?"

I pull the crystal goblet of water towards me that the waiter drops off, bobbing my head. "Yes. I've done ballet for my entire life. Ever since I was old enough to lie," I joke.

Tony nods slowly. "How tall are you?"

"Umm…" My gaze slides to my dad, who is sipping his glass of wine. "Five foot five."

"And you're what… a hundred pounds?"

My neck heats. I look down at the table in front of me, not understanding what is going on. "I don't really know."

"She's full of shit," Hazel says, not even bothering to look up from her phone screen. "She weighs herself every morning. Isn't that right, Kaia?"

I kick her hard under the table. She just smirks at me.

I take a sip of water as I consider whether I should just bolt from the table. The only thing keeping my here at this point is knowing that my dad would probably chase me down and physically force me to come back.

"Would you say you have a lot of boyfriends, sweetness?" the old man says.

For a second, my brow furrows. Who is Tony talking to?

I lift my head and see that he and my dad are staring straight at me. I blink rapidly.

"Excuse me?"

My dad clears his throat. "Kaia hasn't had time for anything other than ballet. Trust me, Tony."

Tony shoots my father such a withering look that I can almost feel it over here. "I'm not interested in hearing your spin on things, Don. I want to hear it from the lady's mouth."

I glance back and forth between my dad and Tony. "I don't think that's an appropriate question. I think maybe I should leave?"

I flush. The last word comes out as a question when I meant it to be a declaration. I start scooting out of the booth as Tony shakes his head.

"Don, control your fucking daughter. This is not going to work if she's gonna be mouthy. The guys at the cat house want a girl that is easy to work with. Nobody likes a smart mouthed hooker."

Cat house? Easy to work with?

Is he… is he suggesting that I… should be a prostitute? Is he considering somehow buying me from my dad?

I'm not sure what they're talking about, but I don't want to stick around to find out. Hazel snickers as I gain my footing and start off toward the entrance.

I put my head down and burst out the front door of the restaurant. My heart beats so loudly in my ears that all other noises are distorted, sounding far away.

I sprint down the block, not making it very far before I hear my dad's voice behind me.

"Kaia Madeline Walker! Stop right now!"

That causes my feet to slow, even though I know I should keep going. As if I'm pulled by some force I can't understand, I turn around.

My father is bearing down on me, his face red and his expression dismal. "Where the fuck do you think you're going?"

My tongue darts out to wet my lips. "Dad, that man seemed to be under the impression that I would be… a hooker."

My dad grabs me by the arm, giving me a violent shake. "He's just trying to make money off of you while you're worth a fucking cent."

I resist when he starts to pull me back toward the restaurant. "Let me go!"

"You are probably spreading your fucking legs for any man that walks by. I might as well be earning a little while you fuck every guy you see."

A frisson of shock and anger shiver down my spine. "Dad, no! Don't touch me."

My dad sneers. "I wish you would say that a little more instead of whoring around town."

I swallow. If he had any actual idea of what I got up to, I would be scared. But I think that my father is just spinning stories to suit his own narrative.

He's done it my whole damn life.

I switch tactics. "OWW!" I scream. "You're hurting me! Help!"

Down the block, I see a couple of police officers turn their heads. My dad sees them at the same time as I do.

His expression goes black but he lets go of my arm. My flesh is mottled around where he gripped me; I already know that it will darken with bruises soon.

"Get back in there, Kaia," my dad says.

I shake my head. "No. No way."

"You'll regret this. If you ever want to see your mom or your childhood home again, do what I say," he grits out.

My eyes fill with tears, but I just shake my head. "No."

With that, I turn and run away, sucking in haphazard breaths.

CALUM

When I see Kaia's face at the top of the escalator, I let out a breath I didn't know I'd been holding. She comes into view, stunning me with her simple clingy black dress and black heels.

I wasn't sure she would come, to be honest. She seemed pretty upset when I dropped her off at her house a couple of nights ago. But here she is, looking up with wide eyes at the enormous light sculpture above our heads. It looks like a great, white jellyfish, its inner light pulsing gently. Against the dark windows surrounding Kaia, it seems like it could be alive.

She takes a step off of the escalator, her eyes pinning me in place. "Where are we?"

I smirk at her a little, holding out my arm for her to take. "Bergdorf Goodman's started a private shopping experience. I thought you would enjoy taking advantage of it."

I start ushering her into the showroom, which is an airy space the size of a normal person's house. It is made up of a runway in the middle, a lounge to the left, and a changing area to the right.

Her eyebrows arch as I guide her to the lounge area. A chicly dressed young woman walks over from the other side of the space. "Hello. I'm Anna. Welcome to the Gallery," she says, bowing her head.

My lips twitch. I glance down at Kaia, noticing for the first time that she seems unusually quiet. "Hi, Anna. I'm Calum. This is Kaia."

"Please, arrange yourselves comfortably," Anna says. Her tone is the perfect combination of a businesslike brusqueness and an easy comfort.

I put a hand on Kaia's back and push her toward a couch, sitting down beside her.

"Can I get you anything? Veuve Cliquot? Fine whisky?"

Kaia's mouth hardens into a straight line. I suck in a breath. "Champagne for both of us."

"Right away," Anna says, hurting off.

I look at Kaia. "You're being oddly quiet."

She turns those killer hazel eyes on me like a spotlight. "I'm sorry," she says, shrugging delicately. "I have a lot on my mind."

I tilt my head, looking her up and down. "Is it something that spending a lot of my money can fix? I brought you here to…" I search for an alternate word for apologize, because I don't want to get in that habit. "Make up for any negative feelings you might have had when we ran into Honor the other night."

For a second, her brow wrinkles as if she's struggling to recall something. "Oh. Wait, we're here for me?"

Her genuine puzzlement is charming.

"Yes, beauty. We are here for you. I thought that you could use a fresh new wardrobe." Tightening my arm around her waist, I wiggle my eyebrows. "I've asked them to pick a selection of their best pieces and some truly scintillating lingerie."

Kaia's eyes widen. "Lingerie?" she gulps.

I have to laugh at that. "Yes, Kaia."

"Oh," she says faintly, looking embarrassed.

Anna comes back with two champagne flutes, handing them to us. Kaia immediately takes a huge sip of hers, trying to hide her red cheeks.

"If you're ready, I'll have the models come out. We will start with outerwear, then move into evening wear, and then intimate apparel."

Kaia ducks her head. I'm not sure why she's so demure all the sudden; last time I saw her, she gave me fuck me eyes all evening.

Well, until Honor showed up.

I clear my throat and look at Anna. "Whenever you are ready."

As soon as Anna is out of earshot, Kaia looks at me imploringly. "You hired models to walk the runway?"

I repress an eye roll. "That's part of the whole reason we are here. You don't have to try anything on unless you want to. We can just order it and then it arrives, perfectly fitted."

Her eyes scan my face. "How much money does an evening like this cost, Calum?"

I shake my head and sip my drink. "You're not allowed to ask that. Just sit back and let me pamper you, beauty."

Her brows pull down but she doesn't argue. All she does is put one of her small hands onto my chest, lean in close, and give me a soft kiss on the mouth. Chaste, yes.

But it arouses me nonetheless, giving me a soft erection. A model struts out onto the catwalk and Kaia turns her attention toward her.

But she also finds my hand with her own, locking her fingers into mine. When she squeezes my hand, I get this weird tightening sensation in my chest.

I stare down at our hands, clasped together on my lap, and something deep inside my chest thaws.

I'm not an idiot who thinks that a stripper is actually into him. I know that Kaia is here for the money.

But I will admit that it doesn't feel terrible to have her cling to me just now. To feel like I'm giving her something she couldn't get anywhere else.

Kaia leans her head close.

"Hey, how do I indicate that I like one of the looks?" she whispers.

I glance up, roused from my thoughts. "Anna!" I bark.

A second later, Anna appears. "How can I help?"

Kaia casts a look back at her. "How do I tell you when I see something I'm interested in?"

Anna smiles lightly. "You can tell me. Or I have placed a card here," she says, stepping forward and handing Kaia a pen and a piece of card stock. "Whichever makes you happy."

Kaia flashes Anna a shy smile. "Thanks. This is my first time here, if that's not obvious."

Anna bows her head. "I think this is a unique experience. Most people haven't been in this private gallery."

Kaia wrinkles her nose. "That actually makes me feel better."

Anna bows her head, receding back. Kaia turns around, taking her hand from mine, and marks something down on the card. She looks at me, smiling a little mischievously.

My lips curl upward at her expression. "What?"

She scrunches up her nose. "I just can't believe I'm here."

I smirk. "This is nothing, Kaia. Just stick with me and I promise, your mind will be blown over and over again."

She rolls her eyes. "Be gentle with me, Calum. I'm easy to impress. Now pay attention to the models onstage, because the outfits I end up wearing are only meant to impress you."

I lean my head over and brush away her blonde hair from the pulse point at her neck. Ever so slowly, I kiss her warm skin, flicking my tongue over it. Then I suck hard enough to leave a mark.

"Calum!" she protests.

"What?" I murmur. "I'm marking my territory. I plan to take my time with you, kissing and sucking every inch of your body until you come on my fucking face."

Her eyes widen; her breath leaves her in an audible huff. She blushes deeply.

"Really, Calum," she whispers, her hazel eyes flashing. "You have the filthiest mouth."

I drop a kiss against her pulse point and then suck on her earlobe. "You have no idea, beauty. Just no idea."

We get a little drunk and watch models strut by. I don't stop touching her, my hands roving up and down her thighs over her dress. I ruck the material of her dress up and run my hands against the hot smooth skin I find there. I drop drugging kisses along her neck and collarbone.

"Calum!" she says, gasping. "There are other people here, you know."

I arch a brow. "And I should care because…"

Her reactions are even better than touching her. She blushes, she laughs, and once I even elicit a breathy moan when I pick a spot close to her nipple and suck.

She shivers. "Calum…"

I'm not sure if it's meant to be a protest or a plea, but it sounds impossibly sweet coming from her lips.

By the time that the lingerie models are walking down the runway, we've opened a second bottle of champagne. I am entirely focused on the woman beside me.

Every little touch, every dirty word I whisper to Kaia is ratcheting up the tension a hair higher. She's pretending to pay attention to the glamorous women wearing frilly lace and black satin that parade themselves down the runway. But the card the she was given has been lost, the pen tossed aside somewhere.

A particularly hot bodysuit made of black straps is the next look coming down the aisle. Calum looks at the model, his mouth lifting at the corners.

He grips my thigh. "I want to see you in that."

I blush, wrinkling my nose. "Well, it'll probably take them a minute to get my size together and ship it from here to Queens…"

"I don't think so. Anna!" he calls.

She appears as though summoned. "How can I help?"

My lips twitch. I jerk my thumb at the model. "Kaia wants to try on looks inspired by that one."

Kaia goes red as a beet, unable to make eye contact with Anna. Luckily, Anna seems prepared for that demand.

"Right away. If she will just step over to the changing area that we have set up, I can bring some options in a moment."

She waves her hand at the silk screens set up on the other side of the room. I arch an eyebrow at Kaia. "Ready?"

She blinks and then starts to move.

KAIA

$\mathcal{A}$nna is already off like a shot. I stand up, smoothing my hands down my dress. Inside, I have a million butterflies fluttering in my stomach.

But I try to take a lesson from Mia, my strip club mentor: hold your head up high and walk like you own the damn place. That's the mentality that I need to come to grips with.

Without saying anything, I start walking over to the area hidden behind the screens. It's actually pretty cute back here, with a pink velour chaise lounge and a free-standing lighted mirror.

Anna knocks and enters with a full rolling rack of black strappy lingerie. "I had a guess at your size. Everything here should fit you but please shout if it doesn't."

My cheeks are red. I sort of expect her to ask some questions about how I know Calum. After all, it's clear that he's the one with the deep pockets here.

But Anna just smiles coolly. "Do you need any

assistance with dressing? Or perhaps another pair of heels?"

Feeling silly, I shake my head. "No thanks."

She vanishes, leaving me alone with the rack of clothes. I mean, if you could even call them that. Looking through the first few items, I would hardly classify the soft silks and chiffons underneath my fingertips clothing.

There are no price tags anywhere, but I'm sure if I knew what any one garment cost I would probably gag. Straps, garter belts, bra cups with a little secret padding… it is for rich people with an elaborate fantasy life. Not for people like me with a job to support their dream of being in the arts.

Pursing my lips, I search through the rack until I come to a very intricate piece I like. Fashioned from white chiffon and dark pink lace, it is a bodysuit that reminds me of one of my ballet costumes. Slipping it free from its hanger, I carry it over to the couch.

I pull up the hem of my dress.

"Stop." Calum's voice stills my fingers. "I want to watch you get undressed."

I turn and find him standing at the edge of the screen, just out of view. Like he's not going to come in if I say no.

I bite my lip and feel a flush rising to my cheeks. This is exactly what he pays me for, nothing more, nothing less. I suck in a deep breath and steel myself.

"Come in," I say softly.

He enters, a hungry look already on his handsome face. He sits down on the pink chaise as casually as you please. His trademark smirk is already splashed across his lips.

"Continue," he directs.

I give my head a tiny shake and start to pull my dress over my head. My hands have the slightest tremor. It feels as though I am baring much more than my body to him.

When I'm left in nothing but the lacy white thong and a matching bra, I toss the dress aside. Calum leans forward, his eyes darkening as he takes in the miles of delicate bare skin I'm offering.

He bites his lower lip for a moment. "Now the bra."

He gestures with a flick of his fingertips. My heart starts pounding. I can't look at him at this exact moment so I brush my hair over my shoulders and turn away.

Unhooking my bra and pulling it down my arms is a matter of seconds. He moves to stand, dragging the couch close to the mirror.

"I want you to watch us," he says quietly. He touches my waist and guides me over to the reflective surface.

There we are, splayed out in the mirror.

I look at the two of us. Calum with his dark hair, in his dark suit, his skin more tanned than mine. He stands behind me and touches my hips, pulling my back half a step into his embrace. His rigid cock digs into my back, a promise and a threat.

I tilt my head as I stare at myself. The blonde who looks back at me is topless, her hazel eyes sparkling softly, her pretty hair covering her tits. His big hands splay out across my torso, coming up to cup my breasts.

I shiver as he pinches my nipples. It is the most bizarre thing, watching myself just now. But I suddenly totally understand why mirrors above beds are a thing.

I watch as Calum hooks his fingers in the waistband on

my panties and skims them down my legs. I blush as the last vestiges of my clothing are removed.

There is nothing between us now, for better or for worse.

He grabs my hips and moves backward to the couch, sitting down. He pulls me down to sit between his legs on a tiny corner of the couch. I can feel the outline of his cock pressing against my ass cheeks.

I just keep watching the slutty blonde in the mirror. He grips my knees and parts my thighs, exposing my pussy. I shudder at that and the blonde shudders too. At the very same time, he kisses my earlobe.

"You are exquisite, beauty." His hand slides down my torso to my mons; his free hand begins to cup one of my tits.

His clever fingers separate my pussy lips and zero in on my sensitive clit. He brushes his fingertips over it, making it throb. I moan softly and arch my back.

But I never take my eyes off of the mirror.

"Calum," I whisper. "That feels so good."

He seals his lips over a spot on my neck, which ratchets up my desire. He doesn't say anything, just makes a mmm sound as his fingertips swirl around my clit.

I reach up to my breasts and put my hand over his, clenching it to my flesh. Showing him what I like in the smallest way.

He responds by gripping my flesh harder, although his fingers on my clit stay relaxed. He nips my neck a few times and uses his teeth on my earlobe.

I let out a shaky moan. Calum chuckles; I can feel the vibrations against the too-hot skin of my neck.

"Do you like that, beauty?" he whispers.

I nod, trying to keep my eyes open. I need him to move his fingers faster over my clit, to increase the pressure. Angling my pelvis, I try to press my pussy into his touch.

"Use your words, Kaia. Tell me how to please you," he rumbles.

"I… I need you to… touch me harder and faster," I gasp. My hips start gyrating as he leans us both back a few inches.

From this angle, the pressure of his fingers against my hot pussy is just right. He starts moving his fingers faster.

"Look at yourself," he says. "Look at how creamy your pussy is, beauty. Look at how bad you want to come."

As he says it, I can feel how ready my body is, feel my pussy growing wetter and wetter. I lean my head back, closing my eyes. Never in my life has anyone else made me feel this way, hot and slutty, ready for him to make me come.

I try to focus on what I'm feeling. My hips are full and heavy, my tits are on fire, my clit aches with need.

"Beg me to make you come," he whispers against my ear. "I want to hear it."

Fuck. I'm close now, I can feel it.

"Please…" I whisper. "Calum, please."

"Please what?"

I push back against him, trying to angle my pelvis more. But he won't budge. He just keeps the same tempo, his fingers damp from my juices.

"Please! Calum… make me come," I demand.

He shifts our bodies subtly, moving his fingers fast. I come suddenly and without warning, my hips jerking, my mouth opening, a growl leaving my chest. My orgasm makes my whole body shudder. Calum just keeps moving his fingers until I reach down and place my hand over his, stopping his movement with a shaking hand.

I open my eyes and immediately kiss him. Open mouth, a little tongue, breathing hard. When I pull back, looking into his deep blue eyes, I make a small confession.

"I've never done that before."

He looks a little surprised. "You've never done what, exactly?"

I flush. "Had someone else make me… come."

He slides his hand along my jawline, burying it in my hair and kissing me deeply. He doesn't say anything in response but I can feel his erection pressing against my back.

This is it, I think. *This is when I finally lose my virginity.*

But when I reach for him, he pulls away. He exhales and shakes his head.

"Not tonight," he says. His expression is all but unreadable as he extricates himself from me. "I'm just going to have Anna send over all this lingerie."

I stand up, glancing at the mirror. "…okay?"

The way I say it, it sounds like a question. But whatever attention he was paying me before, now his body language is forbidding and closed off. He straightens his cuffs and clears his throat.

"I'll leave you to it," he says.

Calum stalks out of the screened area, leaving me to wonder what the hell just happened.

22

CALUM

"No!" I shout. The class full of dancers freezes in place. The piano player falters. "Absolutely not. You are all deeply disappointing. Run that entire piece again."

My words ring out in the studio. The only sounds are the shuffling of feet as the dancers move back to begin again. The piano player starts the movement again, the music swelling and speeding up.

Bas turns his gaze on me, narrowing it slightly. "After this combination, you are dismissed!" he calls out.

I glare at him. He points to his wrist. I'm not wearing a watch, but I would guess that he's trying to chide me. I clasp my hands behind my back and prowl the studio.

When I come to Kaia, I force myself not to stare at her. I just move on though I want nothing more than to pretend that there is no one else in this studio but her.

The knowledge that she gave me one of her firsts — her first orgasm from another person — rests heavily on my heart. I feel conflicted about it…

But also, it's the hottest thing I can imagine. When Kaia closes her eyes and thinks about coming, she can only draw from one experience. Something that I gave her.

I made sure as shit that she had a first time worth remembering. No one should have a terrible memory like I do, in a closet on a pile of coats, with a woman old enough to be my grandmother.

The thought of Anita makes my lips thin.

The combination ends and everybody sags. I purse my lips and glance outside.

"Thank you, everyone," Basil says, clapping his hands.

The sun is already starting to set. I admit that I may have run roughshod over Bas's little schedule. My frown deepens.

I turn around and make eye contact with Kaia. Jerking my chin toward the studio door, I grab my water bottle and head out. I walk to the next studio over, which is empty. Making sure that Kaia sees me, I step through into the emptiness.

It's a couple of minutes before she slips in the door, closing it behind her. Tucking back a loose strand of blonde hair, she raises an eyebrow. "Are you talking to me again, then?"

My eyebrows lower. "If there was a time when I was ignoring you, I'm not aware of it."

Two spots of pale pink appear in the apples of her cheeks. "You have been acting strangely for the last couple of days, Calum."

I repress the urge to roll my eyes at her.

"I wasn't trying to act any particular way." I wave a hand in front of my face. "That's not the reason I want to talk to you. I wanted to know if you would accompany me to a charity gala later."

Her look of surprise is complete. "What? I thought… I mean… you wouldn't want to be seen with me, would you?"

I flash her a smirk. "Relax, Kaia. It's an event that I usually don't attend, with people I normally don't socialize with. No one will know you."

She ducks her head. "I was going to spend the night catching up on laundry."

I reach out and snag her hand, pulling her a step closer. Kaia looks up at me, those hazel depths containing innumerable mysteries. Her gaze sinks to my lips and then to the door behind me.

She sucks in a breath. "If I say yes, can we leave? I don't want to get caught."

I flash her a smirk. "Yes, beauty. I feel the same way."

Her eyes narrow on my face. Her lips quirk. But she doesn't disagree. She just moves back, tugging her hand out of my grip.

"If I want to get home and shower and still meet you out at a reasonable hour, I guess I should take a cab."

She starts to walk away. I reach out and snag her around the waist, pulling her body close to mine. "I'll take you."

"What?" she asks, startled. "No, I don't need you to take me to my house."

I shoot her a hard look. "I said I would take you. Now I'm going to go hit the showers. I'll meet you out front in twenty minutes."

Her delicate throat works as she pulls away from me.

She tosses her hair, raising her chin. "Fine," she says, not a little huffy.

Normally after charging up my batteries like that, I would've spent a little time letting the water run while I stroked my cock. But since I'm pressed for time, I race through my shower and dress in an immaculate bespoke tuxedo. Speeding out the door, I'm still fussing with my bowtie when I find Kaia waiting on the curb.

She's fresh out of the shower too, her hair thrown up in a wet ponytail, her skin glowing. I flag my limousine down as I look her up and down.

There is a part of me that realizes that if I were a slightly different person, if life hadn't fucked me up so badly so early on, I would want to be with a girl like Kaia. Fresh faced, no makeup, no fucking artifice. She's stunning without a face full of make up or a wardrobe of designer clothes.

If I had met her here as a ballet dancer first, without knowing her secret life as Cerise, would I still feel the same?

"Calum," she prompts.

I realize that the chauffeur has opened the back door and is waiting patiently for me to get in. I climb in after Kaia, smelling her honeyed fragrance. I lean closer to her as the door closes, getting another whiff.

It's coming from her damp ponytail.

"That scent… what shampoo do you use?" I ask.

She looks embarrassed. "It's something French. I might have splurged on shampoo and conditioner last week. You don't hate it, do you?"

I let out a bark of laughter. "I love it. You smell just

like a ripe honeycomb. I'm having a hard time not rubbing your scent all over my fucking body."

She grins at that and rolls her eyes. "I'm glad that it meets with your approval."

When we pull up outside of her apartment in Queens, I rake my gaze over her house. It's nothing much to write home about, just a brown brick house that has three stories. Even though it's taller than most of the surrounding buildings, it can't have much square footage.

Kaia opens her car door and gets out. She almost closes the door on me and then looks at me with surprise. "Oh! Did you want to… come in?"

I get out of the back of the limo, buttoning my tux. "I planned on it."

She looks nervously over her shoulder. "Oh. Ummm… all right."

As she leads me up to a door around the side of the house, I look at the neighborhood. From the look of the little Hispanic grocery store on the corner and pedestrian traffic on the street, the neighborhood is mostly Latino. Kaia glances back at me as she unlocks her door, her expression uncertain.

She heads inside, trotting up the stairs. I close the door and lock it, then follow her up. Her space is at once very light and airy, and very small. Nestled up here in the eaves of the house, her bedroom is on the left and her tiny kitchen on the right. Her bedroom is basically a big white bed and a bedside table; I can see that she has a hanging rack of clothes near the wall and a laundry basket beside it. Between the rooms is a gap with shiny wooden floors, probably perfect for stretching.

There is a bathroom in the far corner, it's heavy wooden door pulled shut. And the last thing I notice is a black cat poking it's head out from behind the bed, staring at me with intense green-yellow eyes.

I take the whole room in with a jaundiced eye. I can see that she has a wall of photos pinned up over the bed and a bed for her cat in the corner. Obviously she cares for this space…

"So you live alone," I guess.

She ducks her head, moving to the bed and dropping her duffel bag. "Yes."

Somehow I had imagined her living somewhere more glamorous. I squint around at the room, putting my hands behind my back.

Kaia turns to me, her mouth tugging down. Her cheeks are already stained with color. "It's small. But it gets really good light during the day," she says.

I tilt my head. "I didn't realize that you were struggling financially."

She shoots me a hard look as she goes over to the hanging rack of clothes. "I didn't work at Club X because I liked the camaraderie, Calum."

My lips twitch. "No, I suppose not." I pause, thinking. "Where is your family?"

Her shoulders visibly tense up. She quickly sorts through several dresses, pulling one off its hanger. It takes her a long time to answer my question. "My parents live in Hartford."

I cock a brow. "And why doesn't your family pay for a nicer apartment?"

Kaia turns, her expression baleful. "Not everybody has everything that you have."

I raise my brows at the heat in her tone. "I didn't realize your family was disadvantaged."

She toes off her shoes, her expression pinched, and heads to the bathroom. "They aren't. I grew up with money. It's just… my story is more complicated than that."

She shuts the heavy bathroom door hard, effectively ending the conversation. But her evasiveness doesn't settle anything in my book.

No, it only makes me more curious about Kaia's background.

Walking around her apartment, I notice that she has a number of votive candles, most burned down to the bottom. She also has a box of old pointe shoes in the corner, most pulled apart and scavenged for bits and pieces.

The next thing I see is a small side table with a tray of what appears to be costume jewelry. A cluster of oversized pearls, a diadem with several stones missing. A long chain of intricate silver bangles with several missing links.

"What's with all the broken jewelry?" I call.

"It's not broken! It can still be salvaged. It just needs a little love and attention…" She answers, her voice muffled by the bathroom door.

I pull out my phone, texting my assistant to pull a background check on Kaia and her family. From the look of this apartment, I don't actually know what to think.

There is a mural made of photos that are carefully pinned up by the window. I walk toward it, trying to find some answers.

In the next second though, she steps out of her bathroom again and my mind goes blank. She wears a clingy light blue cocktail dress that shows off her cleavage. She has pulled her wet hair down and it curls gently about her shoulders.

I bite my lip appreciably. Kaia tosses her hair and steps into a pair of dark heels. Then she adds a grey winter coat.

At that moment, I wish I had a diamond necklace to put around her neck and frame her décolletage. Making a note to keep some more jewelry on hand, I exhale deeply.

She turns to me. "Do I need to bring anything?"

My lips curl up. "No. Just yourself. You look utterly intoxicating, Kaia."

She blushes, a little smile playing about her lips. "Thanks, Calum."

I offer her my arm. "Come on. Let's go to the gala and act like we are sophisticated socialites rather than depraved sexual deviants."

She walks over and slides her hand into the crook of my arm. Her hazel eyes glint with a mischievous look. "You take the lead, Calum."

I lean down and kiss her on the lips, hard and passionate. She pushes up onto her tiptoes, kissing me back for just a moment.

It's indefinitely satisfying, the feeling of being wanted by someone as beautiful as Kaia.

Then I urge her toward her apartment steps, thinking of how good that dress will look on my bedroom floor later.

23

KAIA

I suck in a breath as I clutch Calum's arm, my gaze swiveling around the ballroom. A jazz quartet plays in the corner. All the white linen-bedecked tables are pushed to the sides of the room. Inside that, women in extravagant gowns and men in tuxes mill about in the dimly lit ballroom.

Calum leans his head over to me. "Don't be so nervous," he murmurs in my ear.

I swallow and look up at him. "Am I that obvious?"

His lips twitch. "Not to everyone. But I'm the lucky man whose arm you are clutching like it's the only thing keeping you afloat."

I look down and flush. I've got Calum's arm in a death grip and I didn't even notice. Relaxing my hand, I take a breath and apologize.

"Sorry," I whisper back. "I'm just intimidated by all the diamonds and Rolexes I see on the crowd. I thought I was wealthy growing up, but not compared to this room full of people."

Calum flashes me a smirk. "It's just money, Kaia."

I wrinkle my nose at him. "I feel like the only people who say that are already filthy rich."

He makes an mmm sound, apparently not feeling like engaging me on that subject at this moment. Instead he lifts his head, swiveling his gaze around.

"What are you looking for?"

His eyes tighten a little as he slips his arm from my grasp. I open my mouth, about to protest, but he eases his arm around my waist.

"I'm looking for Jack Schwartz. He's the owner of a cryptocurrency modulating software that is particularly ingenious. And I have been trying to buy his company for six months now."

I screw my face up. "A crypto what?"

Calum shoots me a wry smile. "Cryptocurrency. That's how I took a few million, invested it, and came out with enough money to start Indica Tech."

My brows descend. "And Indica Tech… did well?"

He scoffs. "You've got to be kidding. Google, Apple, Indica… we're one of the biggest tech firms out there right now."

I pull a face. "I can barely use my cell phone. I'm not exactly savvy with most of that stuff."

He stops look around the room, suddenly squinting at me. "You seriously just think that billionaires fall from the sky?"

My eyes widen. "Billionaire? Like… you have a billion dollars?"

His lips curve up just a little. "Yes, beauty. My

company is worth several hundred billion dollars. I'll leave you to figure out what that means for me."

I blink up at him. "That's… an incredible amount of money."

He nods, looking around again. He sees the person he is looking for, apparently, because he starts ushering me over toward the other side of the ballroom.

We walk right up to an older man with a thin gray mustache wearing a tuxedo. The man has his arm around a lovely older woman who is wearing a pale purple gown and so many diamonds it's a surprise that she can stand up straight.

They are talking to another couple, but Calum seems unconcerned about that. He elbows his way into their small circle, a broad smile on his face. I've never seen Calum smile like that before, with all his teeth.

It's unsettling and disingenuous, like seeing a shark smile a second before he eats you.

"Mr. Schwartz!" he calls out. "What a surprise!"

Mr. Schwartz blinks a few times and turns toward us. He takes Calum in, his green eyes narrowing. Then he looks at me for a second, dismisses me, and does a double take. His lips part. His eyebrows rise.

"Well, aren't you enchanting," he purrs. He drops his arm from the woman he's holding close and steps toward me. I stand up a little straighter and blink rapidly.

I don't know that Mr. Schwartz even recognizes Calum as a person. He swoops in and takes my hand in his clammy grasp, bowing over it and placing a very wet kiss on the back.

"Enchanté, mademoiselle." He straightens but doesn't release my hand. "Call me Jack. What's your name, doll?"

I lick my lips, nervously glancing at Calum. Calum's lips are pressed into a thin line but he doesn't say anything. So I just incline my head.

"Kaia Walker. It's very nice to meet you."

I manage to wrest my hand from his grasp, stepping back into the shelter of Calum's big body. It had never occurred to me until right this moment to think of Calum as a kind of protection. But now I raise a hand to rest on Calum's back.

Calum clears his throat. "Mr. Schwartz — can I call you Jack?"

Jack is busy looking me over, his gaze seeming calculating. His lips twitch and drags his eyes away toward Calum. Calum extends his hand and Jack takes it, favoring Calum with a look.

"Do I know you already?"

Calum's smile turns hard. "I'm Calum Fordham. I own IndicaTech."

Jack's expression pinches. "Indica… oh, oh. You're with Lucas."

Calum drops Jack's hand, his expression going flat. "Lucas is with me."

He slides his hand around the back of my waist, pulling me closer. It's my first glimpse of Calum being territorial. Actually I'm not sure whether he's more put off by Jack's lack of interest in him or the fact that the other man doesn't know Calum's position.

"Right, right," Jack says, looking back and forth between Calum and me. He rubs his hands together a few times and the purple-gowned woman steps forward and squirts a dab of liquid onto his hands.

Jack smiles, a glint in his eyes. "Did you come here to bring me lovely Kaia as a gift?"

The breath in my lungs freezes. Calum's fingers on my waist tighten. "Very funny," he says, expression growing stony. "I came to meet you face to face because it's been so difficult to set a meeting with you."

Jack looks at me, arching a brow. "You want a meeting with me?"

Calum tilts his head and narrows his eyes. "Yes."

Jack steps forward and runs his finger down my bare shoulder. I don't even know what to do, so I take a half step back. Jack laughs.

"You're fun," he challenges me. "I like them feisty."

"Don't touch her." Calum sounds more serious than I've ever heard him sound before. "I'm interested in purchasing your company, not in sharing my date."

Jack laughs, sticking both of his hand in his pockets and rocking back on his heels. "If she's just your date, that's even better. I thought I was going to have to do some serious haggling to get this little sweetheart in my bed."

"Don't fucking talk to her like that," Calum says, enunciating every syllable perfectly.

I grip Calum's hand, tugging him back. "I think we should go."

"Ah, don't be so uptight," Jack says, waving away Calum's black glare. "I'm just playing around. Unless your little blonde minx wants to fuck in the coat closet?"

Before I even realize what's happening, Calum's fist is

flying towards Jack's face. The rest of the ballroom goes still as questioning glances turn toward us.

The distinct crunch of bone breaking makes my stomach flutter. Jack's face seems to explode, blood streaming everywhere. Then he hits Jack over and over again, in the face and in the stomach, until Calum's fists are red with blood. Jack seems too stunned to fight back, struggling weakly against Calum's onslaught.

"Please! Calum, please stop!" I beg. "Calum!"

At some point, my begging seems to work, because Calum just stops cold. He leans down over Jack, spitting on him.

"I told you not to talk to her like that," Calum hisses through clenched teeth. I scurry forward and pull at his arm.

When he looks down at me, his pupils are as big as dinner plates. He shudders for just a second. I wrap my hands around one of his bloodied fists and tug him back. He falters for a second, then relents.

He turns away, half dragged by me.

Jack is blotting at his nose, which is bleeding profusely. He manages to leverage himself to his feet and shout after us.

"I'm never selling my company to you fucking bastards!"

Calum pauses, his muscles tensing for a fight.

"Please," I whisper, looking at Calum. "Please don't."

Calum looks at me, his sapphire eyes glinting. He looks back. For a second, I think I've lost him.

Then he just sneers and jerks his head toward the ballroom door. "Let's go," he grits out.

I hustle him out of the hotel and downstairs into the icy cold night. The thought occurs to me that our coats are still upstairs.

But that's not important right now.

I look up at Calum, hesitatingly reaching up a hand to touch his cheek. He looks down at me, still breathing hard.

"Are you okay?" I ask.

His face contorts for a moment. "I'm supposed to ask you that."

I squint at him. "I'm not the one who just got into a fistfight, Calum," I say softly.

He brings his hand up to his face, covering mine briefly. For just a second, he closes his eyes and leans into my touch.

My heart starts beating a tattoo in my ears. I can see that he's going through something, but I have no idea where to even begin. I mean, Calum and I are basically strangers, when it comes down to it.

He kisses my palm and steps away from my touch, reaching in his pocket. "Let me call my driver."

Calum starts scrolling through his screen, his expression blank. He puts his free arm around my waist as he dials, looking around.

Consciously or not, he's still in protective mode.

Calum sweeps me along to the street. I watch his face, trying to gauge his mood.

But I can't tell what the hell is going on with him. Especially once the limo pulls up and Calum yanks the door wide.

I get inside with a gulp, unsure what happens now.

24

CALUM

The elevator door dings. Kaia glances nervously up at me as I pause, letting the concierge walk out before us. I stare at her, telling her with my gaze all the things I'm about to do to her.

She shivers and places her hand in mine. I lumber out of the elevator, keeping her by my side.

The concierge smiles at both of us as he walks ahead, sweeping the door open.

"Our most grand suite," he announces.

I walk in, feeling Kaia's small waist against my large hand. I glance around for about three seconds and see everything I need to see: great wall to ceiling views on on side, a lavish sunken living area right ahead of me, a hallway leading off to my right.

The concierge beams. "Will you two require any other—"

I toss my entire money clip at him. "No."

I hear Kaia's tiny intake of breath, watch her hands

close and open. Before the man is even out of the suite, I sweep her up and throw her over my shoulder.

"Calum!" she protests. The sound of her voice is muffled by my broad shoulder.

"Get used to calling my name," I rumble. Shouldering my way through the doorway and into the darkened bedroom, I don't stop until I tumble her to the mattress.

She flexes her hips into mine, leaning up to twine her arms around my neck. I allow myself to be pulled down by her weight. Burying my face in her collarbone, I grab her neckline with both hands and rip her blue dress down to the waist. I expect her to protest again, but she just encourages me, flicking her hips against mine and letting out a needy gasp.

I find her lips with my own, kissing her as hard and as passionately as I can without drawing blood. My cock is pressed between our bodies and one of her hands slides down my neck and over my ribs, making its way toward my zipper.

I growl and grab her hands, pulling them up over her head. In this position, Kaia is under my control, at the mercy of my hungry mouth, my heavy weight on top of her body, my cock throbbing with need. I pin both her wrists with one of my large hands, my mouth ravishing hers, my kiss beyond punishing.

I trail my free hand down her curves to her outer thigh. Gentleness isn't a factor here; I ruck her dress up as hard as I can, loving how she gasps in response. I press her wrists into the mattress, pulling back so I can look down at her gorgeous face.

Her blonde hair is in disarray, her cheeks are pink, her

tempting little breasts in their see through lace bra are heaving. God, she looks so perfect right now, a wet dream come to life.

"Don't move your hands," I grit out. "Tell me you heard me, beauty."

She licks her lips, a quick swipe of her tongue, and nods. "Yes, Calum."

I give her a satisfied smirk, standing up. I pull off my jacket and discard my bowtie, then step out of my shoes. As an afterthought, I pull her heels off and unbutton the top few buttons of my shirt.

She squirms a little as I kneel between her legs, looking down at her tattered dress and the parts of her body I've exposed.

Looking her in the eye, I shred the last bit of her dress and undo the front clasp of her bra. Her breasts are freed and I take a moment to admire them, reaching down and feeling the weight of them in my hands. Kaia arches up into my touch and I reward her by lowering my mouth to her nipple, teasingly kissing my way around it before scraping it with my teeth.

She moans, her hands coming down to bury themselves in my hair. I release her nipple and nip the side of her breast hard. Her whole body shudders as she says, "ow!"

"Put your hands back up over your head," I tell her.

Kaia blinks a couple times and then bites her lip, slowly lifting her hands above her head. I drop a kiss in between her breasts, groaning a little.

"Good girl," I whisper against her overheated skin.

My cock throbs as I slide my body down, hooking my

fingers in the waistband of her tiny thong. I skim her panties down her thighs, pressing my nose into the warm heat of her legs, just below her pussy. She's already wet; I can tell from the stain on her panties and the way the earthy but sharp scent of her pussy rises to my nose.

She whimpers when I pull away. When she pleads with me, her whisper is pure need. "Calum…"

I smirk down at her, unbuttoning my shirt the rest of the way and slipping it off. Kaia squirms again, her hazel eyes darkened with lust.

I grip her hips with my hands, leaning down to kiss her lips again. "What is it, beauty?" I whisper against her warm lips.

Her hips dig into mine as she thrusts. "I need more."

Hearing her innocent plea makes me want to unzip my pants and bury my cock so deep inside her pussy that I may never find my way out again. But I'm trying to take it slow, so I just kiss her hard, working my tongue against hers.

When she moans and writhes against me, I pull back, scanning her face. "I'm going to take my time with you, beauty. The longer you wait for me to fuck you for the first time, the more explosive it will be. And I have all the time in the world… so I'm not going to pop your cherry tonight. I'm going to make you wait a little longer before I pluck your petals, beauty."

The exhalation of her breath leaves her lungs in a quiet moan. I see her hands flex. "Calum…"

I lift myself up and take off my slacks, leaving me bare underneath. Kaia rocks her hips up, her eyes glued to my cock. She sucks in a breath and releases the tiniest groan.

Biting my lower lip hard, I run my hand down to my groin, drawing wide circles around my cock. I look down at Kaia's perfect body splayed out before me.

"Spread your legs for me, beauty," I tell her. "Show me what I'm missing."

Her face heats, but she looks so fucking hungry as she slowly spreads her knees wide, exposing her creamy pussy. I run my free hand inside her thigh, up to her pussy lips. She hisses and rocks her hips against the brush of my fingertips. I circle her entrance a few times, gathering the sticky moisture I find there.

"Does that feel good, princess?"

"Yes," she whimpers. "God, yes."

I fist my cock, staring at her pussy, wet from its own juices. My dick is so sensitive from all this buildup that I can tell I won't last long. So I focus on Kaia, on driving her over the edge.

I trail my fingertips up, spreading the moisture that I've found around her clit. She closes her eyes and hisses as I draw lazy figure eights around her clit and her entrance.

"Bring one of your hands down here," I order her. "I want to watch you touch yourself, dirty little girl."

Her eyes open, piercing me as she draws one shaking hand down the length of her body. She touches her pussy lips oh so gently, her fingers bumping mine as she caresses her clit. She starts to close her eyes again, a little mmm rising from the back of her throat.

"Use your other hand to feel your tits," I say.

She grasps her nipple, tweaking it hard. A shudder of pleasure racks her small frame. I grip my cock, pumping it a few times. Then with the other hand I run my fingers down to her pussy entrance.

I stare at her face. "Look at me, Kaia. I want to watch your expression when I fuck you with my fingers."

Her green-brown eyes open, pinning me in place. Her plump lips part as I tease her entrance. She's slick with want, making it easy to slide one thick digit inside the warmth of her body.

Her expression turns to one of ecstasy mixed with torment. For a moment, I'm afraid that I've hurt her. But she starts feverishly moving her fingers in small circles around her clit.

My body tightens with need. I try to keep the grip I have on my cock light, but my hand is already working my dick over just the way I like it.

I'm determined to get Kaia to the breaking point before I spill my seed all over her pretty body.

"Do you like that, beauty?" I whisper.

She bites her lower lip, her hips thrusting. "Give me more," she says, her voice sultry. "Fuck, Calum…"

I turn my hand so that my palm faces upward and introduce a second thick finger to her tight pussy. I can feel the walls of her channel start to tremble as I begin to work my fingers in and out slowly.

"Oh god," she gasps. "Oh god…"

"Look at me!" I command. "I want to watch you unravel, Kaia."

The second her hazel gaze lands on my face, she starts pulsing, her innermost muscles spasming. Her lower body convulses and her eyes roll up in the back of her head. She lets out a strangled groan, the sound of it like music to my ears.

"Fuck, Kaia," I grit out.

Only a few seconds later I feel my balls draw up and my cock start to twitch. I jet pulses of semen across her lower body, my eyes closing briefly as I come so hard that it almost hurts. I hear a strange sound, only realizing moments afterward that it is a low moan escaping my chest. I desperately thrust a few final times, wringing out every drop of pleasure left in my body.

When I open my eyes and let myself sag onto the mattress beside Kaia, I'm unable to speak. She twines herself around me, seeking my mouth, and I kiss her with lazy flicks of my tongue.

I close my eyes and let myself drift, my arm encircling Kaia's waist, my nose buried in her honey-scented hair.

KAIA

"All right, everyone! Well done." Basil claps his hands, drawing the class's attention. "Today was our last day of classes before we start dress rehearsals for the next two weeks! Final fittings for our costumes will be in a few days so please, no weight fluctuations after that. No pizza, no soda, no salt. I want to see only trim bodies in here."

I blow out a breath, picking up my water bottle from the floor. Looking around, my gaze collides with Calum's sapphire eyes. He arches a brow.

I swiftly look away from him, trying not to blush. It's been a couple of days since he stripped me down and made me come for him. I haven't been able to so much as look at him since then without looking like a besotted school girl.

My eyes widen. The second that he says where the roster is posted, there is a cattle call. Everyone stampedes for the door. I bite my lip and try to avoid Calum's gaze, trickling out among the last of the dancers.

Ella stops me at the door. "I got Princess Florine!"

I give her a startled hug. "Oh! Congrats!"

She smirks. "Shut up. You got the Lilac fairy. You're basically a main player."

My breath seizes up. "Wait, really?!"

I squeal, hugging her. "I can't believe we both got cast!"

She cocks her head at me.

"Of course we did. There are basically almost no more experienced ballerinas above us." Her brow furrows. "Are you feeling okay?"

I smile lightly. "Yeah, sorry. Just off in my own world. I think I need to eat something."

She scrounges around her duffel bag for a protein bar and offers one to me. "Here you go. We can't have you passing out. That would be really bad for everybody."

I accept it, sucking in a deep breath. "Thanks, Ella."

Shouldering my bag, I glance over to see where Calum is. He's already gone; he's spent the last couple of days in meetings, trying to figure out how to keep his business alive now that he's punched Jack Schwartz in the face.

Ella walks out of the dance studio with me, stretching once we are in the echoing hallway. Eric comes up right behind us, grinning.

"Guess what? My friend Crispin has been accepted here. I guess they had too many people that quit."

I tilt my head at Eric. "Oh?"

He wiggles his eyebrows. "Yeah. Everybody that just did the final audition is now a NYB dancer. I mean, until they get yelled at by Calum Fordham, at least."

He rolls his eyes and pulls a face. My cheeks warm a bit.

Ella cocks her head. "When will we get to meet the new dancers? Tomorrow?"

Eric grins, holding up his cell phone. "As it so happens, I just texted Crispin and he said he would meet us outside."

He sounds so excited as we head down the hall. A petty little voice in the back of my head wonders if Eric would be so excited if it was me that had just got accepted.

I can't imagine that he would be. Then again, I think I might have only even gotten in because I'm fucking one of the judges.

I duck my head and blush as we put our coats on and head outside. Now I'm wondering how much of my current career I owe to Calum and how much I owe to years upon years of practice. Did I screw some more talented ballerina out of a spot?

"Crispin!" Eric calls.

I look up and see a group of dancers turn and look over at us. My step falters as I see that Manon is among them, her gleaming brunette hair in a perfect bun, her lilac leotard and hot pink leg warmers looking chic. She notices me right away, her expression going from a smirk to a glare in three seconds flat.

"Uh uh," Ella says, reaching out her hand to pull me to a stop about ten feet away from Manon. She raises her voice. "Don't infect the new guys with your sickness, Manon. No ballet bullies need apply."

Manon crosses her arms, her glare now encompassing us both. "Well, if it isn't Tweedle Dee and Tweedle Can't Dance."

Eric steps in front of us, ready to defend us. But Ella

isn't about to let anyone talk badly about her. She silences him with a gesture.

"You and I have always had a problem with each other, Manon. You don't like my skin color. I don't like trifling little white girls with sticks up their asses. But now you're here at my company, about to trick the new people into thinking you are worth something. I am just not ready for that today."

Manon folds her arms across her chest and tosses her head with a smirk. "And yet, here I am. I'm more talented than the three of you combined, so…"

One of her group steps toward us, sliding Manon a look. He's short and very pale, with pale blond features and a bright yellow track suit on. "I've seen you dance when you were still in the academy," he says, shrugging. "It was only okay."

Eric glances back at me, jerking his head at the guy. "That's Crispin."

Manon regards him flatly. "You only made the cut because you're a teensy, tiny male dancer, okay? Run along now, let the big kids talk."

Crispin's cheeks grow violently red. "You're a fucking bitch!"

"Okay!" I call, motioning to Crispin. "Come on. I have found that with Manon, it's best not to feed the beast. Your hate just eggs her on. Let's go grab a coffee or something."

I hold out a hand and stare at Crispin. He looks at me, taking me in, and swallows. For a second, I think he's going to go right back to yelling at Manon.

But he doesn't. Crispin walks straight over to me, gives me a once over, and then grabs me. I'm taken by surprise when he spins me into his arms and dips me, ending with a passionate kiss.

I freeze as he manhandles me, blinking. This close, Crispin's hands are clammy and his track suit has the distinct odor of moth balls. I bring my hands up and give his chest a push.

Only then does he pull me back up and release me. I stare at him, stunned.

I literally don't know what to make of what just happened, other than the fact that it basically had nothing to do with me.

Manon gives us a sarcastically slow round of applause. "The dork and the dweeb find love at first sight. How nice. You guys should go set the Santa Fe Ballet world on fire."

I step out of Crispin's hold, my head turning to Manon. "Fuck off. I bet you don't last a month at NYB."

She smiles coolly. "I have a sponsor already, so that's unlikely."

"Hey, did someone mention coffee?" Eric jumps in. "I say we go get some and leave this weird playground fight here."

Manon rolls her eyes. "You guys are so fucking lame."

She turns and skips down the front steps, as if she doesn't have a care in the world. I frown at her.

How does Manon have a sponsor before the ballet has even performed for the public?

Crispin offers me the crook of his elbow. "Milady?"

I hesitate for a moment. Ella does me the huge favor of swooping in and dragging me away. "Nope! She's with me." She winks at me. "Come on. Let's go to Heart Coffee. They always have such good matcha."

I mouth thanks to her. She puts her arm around me, giving me a hug.

"That was intense," she says, looking back in the direction of where Manon went.

"Yeah." I wrinkle my nose. "I can't believe I didn't stand up for myself. Not with Manon, not with…"

I slide a look back at Crispin, who is walking arm in arm with Eric.

Ella scrunches up her face. "You do need to learn how to stick up for yourself. I mean, you know I'll always jump in. But I'm not always around."

I bump her hip with my own. She giggles, doing it back to me.

"Maybe you can help me come up with some zingers that I can squirrel away. Just to have some locked and loaded."

She shakes her head, snorting. "It's not about having the words at your disposal. It's more about being ready to verbally spar with anyone, anywhere."

I pout a little. "I wasn't raised with those kinds of defenses."

She gives me a skeptical look. "That's the whitest thing I've heard you say all day. Seriously, that's just straight up a terrible excuse."

My cheeks go pink. "Yes, mother."

She grins, patting her hair. "You wish your genes were as good as mine. We have really graceful arches on our feet and we are all petite and delicate."

I can't argue with that. We walk up to Heart Coffee, jostling and chatting. My phone buzzes when I'm in line; two missed texts from Calum.

I sneak a glance at Ella, then decide not to take a chance. There is no real reason to gamble on getting caught when I can just step outside.

"Hey. Will you get me a small matcha? I'll be right back." I wave a twenty dollar bill in front of Ella's face. "I'll pay for yours, too…"

"Yup." She takes the money. "Hurry back. Don't leave me with these boys."

I shoulder my duffel bag and walk out of Heart, going only a few feet away to the next store. Parking myself against the wall, I look down at my screen.

I WAS THINKING about you for the entire class today, his text reads. Every time I looked at you, I got fucking hard.

I BLUSH and sink my top teeth into my lower lip. Scrolling down, I see an address and a time.

2128 FIFTH AVENUE. 4 PM.

I CAN'T HELP but grin at that. Not only did I make class a little harder for him… but he wants more of me. A little shiver of anticipation slides down my spine as I think of what he could have planned for us in... I look at my watch.

God, I have to be there in under an hour.

"Hey," a woman's voice says.

I look up. I'm surprised to find Honor standing there, looking like a tiny blonde super model in her chic black leather dress and black heels.

I flush. "Hey?"

She shoves a packet of papers at me. I take them, my brow furrowing. "What are these?"

Honor tosses her head, smiling coolly. "I've taken the liberty of calling my contacts in five other cities and finding you a good spot."

I squint at her, tucking a piece of my hair behind my ear. "I'm sorry. What now?"

She crosses her arms, her expression growing impatient. "London. Paris. San Francisco. Seattle. Take your pick of the classical ballet companies. They will accept you into their ranks without you even trying out."

I blink rapidly. "Why would I go to another city?" I ask slowly, confused.

She looks at her tiny gold wristwatch. "Because, dear. Right now you are in my fucking way. You stole my place at NYB."

I shake my head. "I didn't take your place. There were tons of spots to fill once NYB let half the dancers go."

She tilts her head. "I think you bargained with Calum. You offered to fuck him in exchange for a spot in the company." Her lips thin. "That's my spot, as far as I am concerned. And my man. Or didn't you know that Calum has been in love with me for half a decade?"

My mouth opens, but no clever retort pops out. I probably look like an idiot right now. "He is not."

She rolls her eyes. "Yes, he is. And it just so happens that I need him now. So I am offering you a way to escape." She glances up at me, an icy smile playing about her lips. "Or else."

My heart starts beating very quickly. "Should I even ask what you're going to threaten me with? I have to say, if you're here to bully me, you are really late to the party."

H's lips twitch. "I don't threaten. I don't bully." She steps closer to me, her eyes growing dark. "I only destroy. Usually I don't even bother with warning my competition… but you just seem so…" Her gaze rakes over my body. The mockery in her tone makes me feel ashamed, somehow. "I was going to say delicate, but that's not the right word, is it? No, I think it's more like easy to crush."

I swallow, shaking my head. "I think you need to take these papers back, Honor."

She reaches out and picks a speck of lint off my shoulder. "Keep them. Read them over. My offer only lasts for the rest of this week. After that, you'll be lucky if I let you live out the month."

With that, she turns and struts away, soon vanishing amongst the crowd walking down the Manhattan street. I blink, looking down at the papers.

Then I remember Calum's texts.

What am I supposed to say?

Hey Calum, your would-be girlfriend just threatened to kill me if I don't leave New York? Could we maybe make it another night?

"Here," Ella says, thrusting the to go cup in front of my face.

I startle a little, looking at her with wide eyes. She nods at the cup. "I am not that sneaky. You're just ten kinds of jumpy today. Here, take it!"

I manage to juggle the papers in my hands and stick out my hand for the tea. She hands it over and takes a spot up against the wall, sipping her tea. Her eyes roam the sidewalk.

"Yo, the new dude gives me weird vibes," she comments.

"Oh?" I ask.

"Yeah, let me tell you why…"

She launches into the topic. I should probably listen, because he gave me weird vibes too.

But I am much, much more worried about the threats Honor just made… and how Calum is going to react.

26

CALUM

I stand in the apartment I've bought just for seeing Kaia, staring out at the Manhattan skyline. The lights are starting to flicker on. It's the deepest part of winter and the sun will be down soon.

Behind me, the apartment is decorated lavishly. A huge white bed takes center stage, a stripper pole is set up one one side, and a whole wall of sex toys faces it from the opposite end of the expansive room.

Everything is just where I want it.

But looking around this incredibly expensive space makes me think of Kaia's apartment. How opposite the two places are, how diametrically opposed.

Maybe that's the next step. I can offer to have Kaia move in here for a while. Turning to look around the space, I sigh.

It would probably be better if I offered to let her redecorate the place too. It's a perfect fuck palace right now but I doubt Kaia would actually want to live here…

Right on cue, Kaia appears through the large front

door. She's wearing a short yellow dress and one of the coats that I bought her from Bergdorf Goodman. Her cheeks are bright pink from the cold. She ducks her head and comes over to me, leaving her purse on the bed.

"You summoned me," she says shyly, smiling just a little.

My lips twitch. "I did." Walking over to her, I reach out and take her by the waist, pulling her against my body. She drops her head back, looking at me expectantly.

I cup her jaw, flick my gaze down to her lips, and ever so slowly kiss her. Her lips are warm. Her warm honey scent rises to my nose, enveloping me.

I grip her tighter. This girl drives me insane without even really trying. If I weren't so fucking broken, I would be thinking about making a longer term arrangement with her. A year, maybe.

When she finally pulls back, her lips bee-stung and her hazel eyes glimmering, she offers me another shy smile. "I think there is something that I should tell you about."

I push out a long exhalation, taking her by the hand and leading her over to the bed. Kaia looks at the bed and glances at me, biting her lip. I can see her doing the math.

"I'm not about to fuck you," I tell her bluntly. "Even though your dress tells me I should think twice…"

I sit down on the bed, pulling her down onto my lap. She straddles me, sucking in a breath. I kiss her, unbuttoning her coat and pushing it off her arms.

"Calum…" she says. The way she says it, a warning mixed with a plea, says that she wants me.

I can feel it in the way her hips press against mine. Smell arousal coming from her body. Taste it on her lips.

Good. That's just how I imagined it would be in the days before I finally fuck Kaia. I nip at her lower lip, digging my hands into her hair.

God, she makes my cock so fucking hard.

"What were you saying?" I whisper, my tone teasing.

She surprises me by putting both hands on my chest and pushing me back. I gaze at her, arching a brow.

She flushes. "I have to tell you about the run in I just had with Honor."

It takes my lust-filled brain a few seconds to make the correct connections and change tracks. I clear my throat. "What now?"

Kaia eases herself off my lap and onto the bed beside me. "I was just walking down the street, minding my own business when she confronted me. She gave me the phone numbers of a bunch of ballet companies in other cities. She said to call the one I wanted and they would take me immediately."

I narrow my gaze on her face. "That doesn't sound like Honor."

Kaia screws up her face. "She said that she wants her spot in the company back. And that she wanted… well, you. She said she wants to date you."

My mouth opens. I try to digest that information. "I… she… what?"

Kaia wrinkles her nose. "She said I was in her way. And if I didn't transfer this week, she would… kill me?"

The end of her statement turns into a question. I squint, trying to make sense of what Kaia is telling me. "Honor threatened you?"

She ducks her head and nods. "Yes."

"And she said… that she wanted her place back at the company?" I repeat.

She nods. "Yes. She accused me of stealing it. She also said that you are the only reason I got the position."

My mouth pulls down into a frown. "That's not true."

Kaia rolls her eyes. "I think you're focusing on the wrong thing. She really wants her spot back. And she wants you on her arm as well. She's willing to make threats over those things."

I reach out, sliding my hand along Kaia's jaw. "I wouldn't take her seriously. Even if she feels that way, the NYB would never take her back. And I'm… preoccupied."

The last part sounds stiff. Puzzlement flashes across Kaia's face.

"Preoccupied?" she echoes.

Jesus. The last thing I wanted today was a referendum on whether I'm happy with the woman I'm basically paying for sex. I close one eye, screwing up my face.

"I am content with how things are," I say. "I call you, you come over, we both have a little fun."

She squints. There is no way of telling how my statement landed. She is quiet for a moment then she clears her throat.

"So what should I do about Honor?"

I shrug a single shoulder. "Nothing. I'll deal with her directly."

Her eyebrows lower and a frown tugs at her lips. "That's it?"

I reach out and grab her by the waist, pulling her closer. "I promise. I'll take care of it. You have nothing to worry about, okay?"

Her mouth pulls into a thin line. "Okay…"

My lips twitch. "It doesn't sound like you trust me."

Her cheeks go bright pink. "I didn't say that."

I look down at her, brushing a lock of her hair back. "You should have a little faith, beauty."

Her eyes scan my face as she bites her lip. I wait patiently while she makes up her mind.

"Okay," she says at last. "I will."

One corner of my mouth kicks up into something resembling a smirk. "Good. Now are you ready for your present?"

Her eyebrows hunch. "My present?"

I bite my lower lip. "Yes. You will have to perform for me first, though. It's been a while since you stripped for me, beauty."

Her eyebrows raise slightly. "That's it? I just told you I was threatened by Honor."

I quirk my lips. "And I'm telling you to forget about that and dance for me."

She narrows her eyes but gets off the bed, taking her heels off. I get the idea to jump up and grab a pair of vibrating panties off the wall.

I wiggle my eyebrows at her as I make my way back to the bed and sit down. "I want you to wear these, Kaia."

I hand them over to her and watch as she draws the silky waistband apart. It takes her a second to figure out what they are.

"Are these…" Her intense hazel gaze sweeps up to me. "Is there a vibrator in these underwear?"

I grin and lay back, putting my arms behind my head.

"I want you riding my lap and begging to come first. Then I'll give you my present."

She licks her lips nervously.

I tilt my head. "You're supposed to trust me, remember?"

Two spots of heat appear in her cheeks. She just nods, turning around. She shimmies out of her white lace thong and steps into the bright red one instead.

She turns around, a little perplexed. "I don't know how you turn it on…"

I smirk and hold the tiny remote control up for her to see. "Don't you worry about that, beauty. Just come here first and sit on my fucking lap like a good girl."

She pales at that, sucking in a breath. She comes up to me, hesitantly trailing her fingers along each of my knees. "Is there music?"

A simple tap of my phone is all it takes and then notes burst into the air. I reach down and adjust my hard on, which is tenting my pants.

"Come on, darling," I whisper.

Kaia straddles my lap, sinking down on top of my cock. As soon as she presses her hips against mine, squeezing my cock that is wedged between our bodies, I hit the on switch.

Kaia actually squeals, her eyes widening as the vibrating panties start to do their work. I don't miss a beat. Taking her hand, I slide it down between our bodies until it touches the vibrator.

"Show me how good you are, Kaia. Guide it to your clit," I command.

Her hazel eyes land on me for a moment. She licks her

lips again and then moves the vibrator lower. I know when it hits the right spot because her whole body shudders with sensation, her eyelids sinking halfway closed.

Kaia gives the breathiest moan. I unzip my dark slacks, reaching in and pulling out my rigid cock. Her breathing hitches as she watches me stroke myself up and down a few times.

Her eyes flit up to meet my gaze. "Can I… I mean, I've never touched one…"

"You want to know how to stroke my cock, beauty?"

She flushes a little. "Please?"

I draw in a deep breath. Until now, I've always been the one in control, always been the one giving myself pleasure. It's usually better that way.

Easier for me, anyway. Less messy, less… emotionally entangled.

But here, with Kaia looking at me so innocently, I nod slowly. "Leave your hand on the vibrator. I want you to make yourself come, Kaia. But if you want to feel my cock, I won't say no."

Taking her free hand, I fold her fingers around my cock, mimicking my own grasp. At first, it feels odd. Having someone else touch me is…

Unusual.

But soon I force myself to relax, closing my eyes. I keep my hand over hers, guiding her tempo and grip. It feels fucking good.

I open my eyes and look down at her working the vibrator against her clit. "You want it to go faster, beauty?" I grit out.

She bites her lip. "Can it?"

Her eyes widen as I turn the remote up two clicks.

"Oh! Fuck, Calum!" she says. "Jesus, that feels so good…"

I slow my hand, gently removing hers. Then I fist my cock and work my fist up and down my length with punishing speed. "Tell me how much you want me to fuck you, Kaia. Tell me what you think about when you're in bed alone, touching your clit…"

God damn. This is so much better already than jerking off alone by myself, thinking about Kaia sucking me off.

Her eyes drift closed. Her legs spread a little wider. "You, Calum. I think about you. I wonder… I wonder what it will feel like the first time you stretch me out…"

That image is too powerful for me. I come suddenly and without warning, shouting her nickname.

"Fuck, beauty! Fuck!"

I thrust upward, pulsing my release out onto her stomach, guiding our bodies together. For a second, I can't even think or speak.

I come back to myself after half a minute to find Kaia still splayed out on my lap, pressing the vibrator against her clit and rocking her hips against it.

I withdraw the necklace box from my pocket, cracking it open. Inside lies a thin platinum chain, hung with the most exquisite diamond pendant I've ever seen.

Kaia pauses when she lays eyes on it, her body freezing up. "Calum, I—"

I shush her, moving her hair aside and clasping the necklace around the slim column of her throat. She touches the pendant, awestruck. "It's beautiful."

I pull her down to kiss her lips, pressing her whole body against mine. "Just like you. Now just relax…"

I flick the remote, turning it up two more notches. The panties are now vibrating so hard that I can feel it buzzing against my thigh.

Kaia closes her eyes and kisses me desperately, needing to come. She thrusts and rocks her hips, her fingers pressing the vibrator into her clit.

"Oh, I'm going to—"

She spasms violently, her whole body convulsing, her mouth dropping open. She howls with pleasure, panting when she's done riding the wave of ecstasy. Only then do I turn off the device.

Only then does Kaia open her eyes, dropping a kiss on my lips. We lay together like that for a long time, drifting, unwilling to break the intimacy of the moment.

KAIA

"No sucking in your stomach!" Gus, the elderly costumer, reminds me for the sixth time.

I scrunch up my face. "Sorry, Gus."

He tuts and goes back to fidgeting with something very close to my butt. I pull myself upright, so I look grand standing on a three foot tall step stool, trying hard to keep my body shape the same. No sucking my stomach in, no letting my back and ab muscles relax either. It's a special kind of torture, I'm pretty sure.

Looking at myself in the mirror, I cock my head. The woman standing before me seems so slender beside the portly Gus. I'm dressed head to toe in shimmering fabric. My tutu is a dark purplish red, the bodice of it stark white. Trailing down and crossing my whole body are the most delicate, intricate lilac flowers I've ever seen.

That part makes me smile. I am the Lilac fairy, after all. I'm dancing the part of the fairy that saves Sleeping Beauty — or gets as close as she can, anyway.

I bite my lip, unable to suppress a little grin. I'm content.

No, more than that.

I'm happy.

Rehearsals start soon. I've told Calum about H's threats and he has promised to deal with them. And on top of all that, I think Calum will finally seal the deal soon.

This could be my last week as a virgin. And I honestly cannot fucking wait.

"Too much belly!" Gus snaps.

"Oh, sorry, sorry!" I try to suck it in just enough. "Is that okay?"

Gus doesn't answer, he just hmmphs. As I stand perfectly still, staring at myself, I start to imagine people in the mirror. Specifically I see my father heading down the hall, his face set in a stoic pout. I wrinkle my nose at that.

Of all the people to conjure, I chose him? I close my eyes and try to keep myself perfectly still.

It's not until my father actually growls at me that I realize that he's really here, in the fitting room with me.

"Kaia!" he barks.

My eyelids snap open. I take a half step back, only to be reprimanded by Gus.

"What are you doing!?" he hisses.

I can't take my eyes off of my father. He is glaring at me, his fists clenched, his jaw locked.

"Do you want to have this conversation here?" my dad asks.

I swallow and shake my head. We are on my turf, so I feel safe enough talking to him… and there is the fact that

I don't want anyone to know just how little my own father thinks of me.

"We're going to have to finish this fitting later, Gus," I say.

Gus shoots me a glare. "You cannot leave right now."

I step down, only vaguely even aware of Gus's presence. "I'll be back."

Behind me, Gus throws up his hands in a baffled gesture. "You have pins all along your back! Don't even think of sitting down!" Gus yells at my back.

Eyeing my dad, I head out of the costume room and take a right into a long backstage passage. Leaving behind the bright light and airy space of the costume room, I advance down the dimly lit, cramped hallway.

My father is right on my heels, grabbing my arm and jerking my body around to face him. His fingers dig into the flesh of my upper arm. "I've been calling you," he says.

I swallow, my gaze raking his face. All my life, I've been conditioned to say yes, to give away what little I have to make my father happy.

But no more. Lifting my chin, I try to keep my tone even. "I haven't been picking up because the last time I saw you, you tried to sell me."

My father bares his teeth. "And if you had just been reasonable then, this whole situation would be resolved right now. But as it stands, things are so, so much worse."

I try to wrest my arm from his grip. "Let go of me. You are hurting me."

He squeezes my arm even tighter, his touch brutal.

"Good. You need to listen this time instead of running away like a little girl."

I pull back, affronted. "I am your little girl!"

His face contorts with rage. He gives me a hard shake. "Shut the fuck up and listen to me, you stupid, worthless whore. You and I are going to leave right now and go back to Tony. And we are going to beg for him to take you."

I shake my head, my face heating. "No! Why would I do that? Why would I do anything for you when you treat me like this?"

My father grits his teeth and pulls me in close, talking low. "Because, Kaia. I owe a lot of money to some very bad people. And either I make good on their investment, or they start looking for ways they can take their money back. They have made that crystal clear. And I don't think your mother would make it very long as a hooker."

My jaw drops. "What?!"

My head spins. My dad is talking about my mom as if she's just another of his possessions. I can't wrap my head around the idea that my dad owes so much money that he's lining up me and my mom to sell off like we're cattle.

Of course, there is no mention of my dad working off the debt or my sister being involved in any way.

My dad takes a step forward, pushing me back against the wall. "If I don't come up with three hundred thousand dollars in the next two days, I will have no choice but to sell your mother and your sister to the mafia. With you, I've worked out a sweet deal. But your mom and your sister are not worth nearly as much. Do you want to know what kind of life you're consigning them to, Kaia?"

"That is such bullshit!" I yell, pushing him back a step.

"This is your mess! You should have to clean it up, not me and not your family!"

My dad's eyes go black. He flings me against the wall, pressing the pins in my garment into the skin of my back. Then he puts both his hands around my throat and starts choking me.

I flail, my eyes going wide, my airway suddenly obstructed. I try to swat at my dad's hands, my fingernails finding the flesh of his forearms.

But that only makes him more angry. "If you won't come with me, you will be punished. I paid for everything for you growing up. And I will be repaid for it all or I will kill you."

My vision starts to swim. I try to call out, try to kick at my dad's legs. But I am powerless against him, struggling mindlessly.

"Kaia!" comes a familiar shout. "What are you doing—"

Calum steps into the passage, looking aggravated. It only takes him a second to register that I'm in danger.

"What the fuck?" he shouts, rushing at my father and me headlong.

My dad takes his hands from my throat, throwing them up in self-defense. "Mind your own business!"

Calum doesn't even hesitate or flinch. He just barrels straight into my dad, tackling him to the ground. "Go get some help, Kaia!"

My dad starts to fight back. I put my fingers on my throbbing throat, still in shock.

Calum grits his teeth. "Kaia! Now!"

Tears begin to fill my eyes and I turn, stumbling down

the passageway. I turn toward the costume room, my mind racing.

Luckily Basil comes down the brightly lit hallway, looking up with alarm at my disheveled state.

"Help!" I shout. It comes out sounding strangled but it's enough to get Basil to rush over to me.

"What's going on?" he asks.

"Calum has tackled… an intruder," I gasp out.

Basil looks confused for a moment, pushing past me. A couple of dancers appear from the costume room, trying to see what the fuss is about. Bas reaches the passage and sees the two men fighting.

"Fuck! Call 911," he calls, rushing to help Calum.

One of the dancers whips out a cell phone, calling the police. I back up as she rushes past me, trying to tell why she's calling the cops.

I lightly touch my neck, feeling my father's hands still choking me.

"He's getting away out the side exit!" someone yells. "Someone stop him!"

I lean down, feeling dizzy.

"Kaia? Are you okay?"

I nod even as I burst into tears, my face going red.

"Someone get the nurse!"

I hear Calum's voice again. "He ran outside. I'm not going to give chase."

I look up tearfully and my gaze connects with Calum's deep blue eyes.

"Shit," he says. He heads over to me, kneeling next to me. "Kaia, are you okay?"

I want nothing more than to collapse into his arms, a weak, broken thing. But I can't do that.

Even now, I'm aware of that.

So I just nod, ashamed at how fragile I feel right now. Calum licks his lips, not touching me, and tries to calm me down.

"It's going to be okay," he says, his voice soothing. "He won't get away."

I look at him, my expression pleading, although I don't know what exactly I'm asking him to do. "He's... my father..."

Calum's eyes widen. He glances back over his shoulder, his mouth thinning. "Okay. It's... it's going to be okay."

He clenches his fists, looking over his shoulder again. "Can we get her a blanket or something?"

As I stand there, shivering, I look at the man in front of me. And I realize how much more it would mean if only he could hold me when he assures me it's going to be okay...

"Kaia!" Ella shouts, jostling through the suddenly crowded hallway.

I turn my head. She opens her arms to me and I am drawn to hug her like a magnet finding its mate. I bury my head in her shoulder, my tears falling.

She rocks me back and forth, making soothing noises. "It's okay, baby. It's okay..."

When I glance to find Calum again, he has vanished, leaving me aching in a way I cannot explain.

CALUM

It takes the police two hours to arrive and take statements from everyone. I make sure to tell the officers that arrive on the scene what I know — that Kaia said the attacker was her father. Then I feel restless enough to have my assistant call the chief of police.

There is no way that I'm going to let this drop. I'm still shaking with rage, even when the police officers offer Kaia a ride home. She looks at me, as if seeking permission.

I shake my head subtly.

Like hell I'm about to let strange men give her a ride anywhere.

I make my exit fairly quickly and have my limousine waiting around the corner when Kaia finally manages to shake off all her well wishers. Her friend Ella stays with her until the last minute, only leaving when Kaia seems to insist.

By the time she slides into the back seat with me, my nerves are completely blown. I turn to look at her. I'm not even sure what to say.

I suck in a deep breath. "It's going to be okay, Kaia."

She looks at me, seeming shellshocked. "Is it?" she asks faintly.

I lift an arm, encouraging her to hug me. Her brown-green eyes fill with tears again and she scoots over, wrapping her arms around my torso and burying her head against my chest. She sobs silently for a minute as the limo pulls away from the curb.

I look down at her small shoulders, shaking as her tears soak my shirt. I barely recognize this person, this broken spirit that's clinging to me just now. If I had been able to see into the future at Club X, would I have chosen this girl?

Hell no.

But now I feel sort of protective of her in a way I can't explain. After all, no one else is looking after her best interests.

No one but me, as fucked up as that might be.

"I'm going to take you to my penthouse, beauty," I tell her gently.

She doesn't really acknowledge that I've even spoken, but her tears do lessen as we drive. By the time we get out of the limo and I bundle her into the private elevator, she's not holding onto me anymore.

Kaia does hold my hand though, looking blankly at the mirror reflecting a distorted version of herself back at her. I finding myself wondering what it is that she sees.

I doubt it's anything beautiful.

The elevator dings and the doors open into the perfect white waiting room. I guide her through the door at the far end, into the darkly furnished living area. I drop her hand

and grab her shoulders, steering her toward the hallway at the very back. It's only another minute before we are in one of the guest bedrooms; my own bedroom, at the other end of the apartment, seemed a little too intimate for this moment in time.

"Sit down," I say, pointing to the bed.

She blinks, casting her gaze around the well appointed yet rather dull looking room. Everything is gray, from the lamps to the bedspread, the bedside table to the armoire. Kaia moves to the bed and perches on one side, her movements lacking in her usual grace.

She looks pale, as if she's been bled dry.

I stand above her for several long seconds, trying to decide what I'm supposed to do with her. I'm out of my depth here, traveling in a strange and emotion-laden place.

"I'm going to run you a bath," I announce after a second.

She looks up at me, nodding. I can see the redden marks on her neck and on her arm.

My fists close, spasming involuntarily. I feel... helpless.

I don't like it at all.

Spinning, I walk purposely into the en-suite bathroom, yanking the taps of the clawfoot bathtub. As the bathtub fills with steamy water, I turn to look at myself in the mirror. There is a smear of blood on my cheek and a faint reddish mark just below my right orbital bone.

A reminder that her father is a very real threat. I didn't learn his name... I make a note to ask my assistant for the file that I had the private investigator put together.

When Kaia appears in the doorway behind me, hesitant, I turn toward her. She is wearing a pair of baggy sweats, pushed on her by Bas in lieu of the tattered costume she was wearing when I found her.

I motion for her to come in. "Close the door."

She does it meekly, without saying a word. I walk over to her and tilt her chin up.

"You're okay," I tell her. "It's over."

Her eyes are glassy. She looks at me for a moment, then looks away. "It's not over. Not really. My father has my mom and my sister to use as leverage over me. It's been this way my whole life."

I frown. "You're safe," I tell her softly.

Kaia looks at me sharply. "You don't understand. That back there? That's who my father is. That's why I live in such a tiny apartment. Why I work at Club X. Can you just…"

She stops, taking a deep breath and dropping her gaze. "Please stop trying to make things okay. They aren't really ever going to be okay."

I slide my hand under her jaw, forcing her to look at me. "I'll never bend. Never become flexible and pliable. Never be soft and malleable. But I think that happens to be just what you need right now, beauty."

She studies me, her throat working. "I'm so tired, Calum."

I nod. "I know."

I reach down and unzip her hooded sweatshirt, peeling it off her lithe body. She toes off her shoes and lets me push down the waistband of her sweatpants. When she stands naked before me, shivering against the steamy air, I guide her to the bathtub.

Acting a steady frame for her to hold onto as she climbs in, I kneel as she sits down. The hot water sloshes for a moment as she settles in with a sigh.

I trail my fingers through the water as it continues to fill the tub. Kaia closes her eyes.

Reaching for the lavender scented soap, I dunk it under the water and then start to lather her arms, her knees, all the places that aren't sensitive. She releases a sigh at one point but doesn't say a word.

She stops me for a second, bringing her wet hand to my face. Using the gentlest touch, she rubs away all the traces of blood, washing them away like they never existed.

I wash her hair next, sliding my hands through the silken strands. She seems to fall into a trance as I rub circles into her scalp, even moaning once or twice.

By the time I am done and her hair is rinsed, she looks at me with a sigh. Her eyelids are heavy, her voice low and rough. "Thank you."

My lips tip up at the corners. "You're welcome."

She inhales a long breath, shaking her head. "I don't mean for washing my hair, although that was nice. I mean… thank you for jumping in today. You probably…" Her eyes close briefly. When they flutter open again, they are filled with tears. She takes a steadying breath. "You probably saved my life today, Calum. I promise, I won't forget it."

Then she does the oddest thing. She takes my hand, still wet from the bath, and turns it over. She places the lightest of kisses right in the middle of my palm.

Something breaks loose deep in my chest. A chunk of ice in the very cold, very dark ocean that is my heart.

I stare down at her. She looks up at me.

I tilt my head and move closer. She turns her face up toward me, seeking my lips.

When we kiss, there is no hint of gentleness, no sweetness to be found.

Only cloying desperation.

I lift her from the bathtub and carry her into the bedroom, unaware of anything but the need to be inside her.

KAIA

*D*ripping wet, wrapped in Calum's strong arms, I kiss him desperately as he carries me into the bedroom. He doesn't stop until he tumbles me down onto the mattress, looking down on me, his breath coming in ragged pants.

"Stay here," he commands. "Stay just like that, beauty."

Calum turns and disappears out the bedroom door for a moment, his footsteps receding into silence. Seconds tick by. I grow restless.

What is he doing?

But soon enough, he returns. He's holding a golden roll of condoms in one hand. He doesn't mention them as he places them on the bedside table.

Then Calum focuses on me, reaching out to touch my knee. He spreads my knee out for just a moment, using his free hand to grip my opposite hip. My pussy is partially exposed and he brushes his hand over my lower lips ever so briefly.

I shudder, anticipation already building.

"Oh, beauty," he rumbles. He looks up at me, our gazes clashing. "The things I'm going to do to you…"

He starts to rip off his loose t-shirt, whipping it over his head and exposing his chest, abs, and arms. Every part of Calum is more impressive than the last; he could truly be a statue carved of marble, come to life.

He hooks his thumbs in his black sweatpants and shoves them down, kicking them off. For a second he is bare before me, standing proudly, his cock jutting out. His expression is dark, his gaze feral. It's like being observed by a big cat who keeps licking his jaws, indicating that it's time for dinner.

I'm his sole focus right now… and I'm ready for his hands all over my body. Ready to gasp and writhe and know the pleasure that he means to give to me.

I shiver, sitting up, and reach for him. Curling my fingers around the firm flesh of his hips, I pull him down. He pushes me onto my back and our legs tangle. His cock presses into my lower belly as his full weight comes to rest on me briefly.

My breath leaves my lungs in a gush. Calum's blue eyes scan my face as he bites his lip. He thrusts against me once as he kisses the left corner of my lips. I writhe against his body, moaning softly.

He takes the weight of his upper body off mine, transferring it to his arms. I lock my legs around his waist, biting my lip as I run my hand down between us. When I reach the tip of his cock, smoothing my palm out to touch it gently, he sucks in a sweeping breath.

"God, Kaia," he whispers. He thrusts against my hand,

biting his lip. "Do you feel how hard my cock is? Hmm? You make me this way." He leans his weight on one arm, reaching his hand up to cup my jaw hard. "I'm going to pop your cherry tonight, beautiful. But before I use my big, hard cock to stretch you out, I'm going to make that pretty little pussy cream for me."

My breath hitches. I feel a trickle of desire escape my entrance. Looking at Calum's expression, I have no fucking doubt that he means it.

I groan, my impatience growing, and rock my hips against his body. "I want to feel you inside me."

Calum smirks and drops a kiss on my lips. "Patience, beauty."

I wrinkle my nose at him. Sliding my hands between our bodies once more, I touch his cock, which is hot against even my warm skin. He hisses, closing his eyes briefly.

"Be careful what you wish for, Kaia." He eyes flicker open, seeming to pierce me down to my soul. "You just might get it."

I shoot him a defiant look and wrap my small fist around his cock, working it up and down his length. He grabs my hands up pins them up above my head, growling.

"Tonight is supposed to be about you," he grits out.

My eyebrows quirk. I'm a little breathless when I finally speak. "It is about me, Calum. I want to learn everything about what makes you feel good." I bite my lip, hesitating. "Teach me, Calum. Don't hold back. I want to learn."

His pupils are so large by now that when he casts his gaze over me, they are nearly black with desire. "Oh, princess. Do you know what you're asking me to do to you? I've spent the last month dreaming of that pretty mouth wrapped around my cock. Of you being a good little girl and holding still while I fuck your face…"

My eyes widen. "You have?"

He nods, his hand wandering down to frame my breast. He tweaks my nipple, causing a shockwave of sensation to slam my oversensitive body. I throw my head back, groaning.

Calum lumbers to his feet. He gestures to me, his gaze like a burning brand over my naked body. "Come to me on your hands and knees, beauty."

I roll over and then push up, turning and moving toward him. He groans as I approach.

"Do you know how fucking hot you are right now?" he growls.

I stop when I reach the edge of the bed, shaking my head slowly. His cock juts out proudly from his body. He steps closer, brushing his lower thighs up against the bed.

I reach out to take his cock in my hand, looking up at him for guidance. Our gazes clash and he shivers.

"Fuck," he says. He lets me explore for half a minute more before pushing my hand away, fisting his cock in his hand.

His gaze drops to my mouth. He tilts his head, giving himself a lazy stroke.

"Open your mouth, sweetheart," he rasps.

I lick my lips and open my mouth. He runs his free hand through the mass of my hair and then grips it, guiding me forward.

The last thing I see before my face is buried against his

skin is a drop of milky white semen leaking from the crown of his cock.

"Put your tongue out," he coaches.

I stick my tongue out and he prods it with the tip of his cock. It tastes salty and metallic, the skin as soft as velvet against my tongue. But as soon as I adjust to that, he is tugging on my hair, lifting my throat.

And then he nudges his cock into my mouth, inch by slow inch. I try to put my hand up, to give myself a little control over how fast he moves, but he knocks it away.

"Don't," he grates out. "Just cover your teeth with your lips and try to relax."

Looking up at him, my head gripped by his hand, I cover my teeth and relax as much as I can.

Calum keeps pushing his cock inside my mouth, the tip almost brushing my throat. I can't help but gag, my whole body shuddering at once.

"Fuuuuck," he says, watching as I try to control the reflex.

He flexes his hips again, forcing his cock to touch my throat. I gag again, throwing my hand up to drag myself backward with a gasp.

A loud sound bursts forth from his chest, a rumbling bass growl.

He steps back, pulling his cock out of my mouth with a pop. I look up at him, sucking in my breaths.

Calum strokes his cock, looking at me. "So much to do, so little time." He bites his lower lip and cocks his head. "I like watching you gag on my dick, princess. But now I need you on your back. I'm going to taste your sweet pussy and make you come on my tongue."

My eyes widen. "Is that a promise?"

He pushes me forcefully onto my back and then comes down to rest on top of me. He drinks me in with his eyes, growling softly as his fingers trail down to stroke my dripping slit.

"God, Kaia. You're so fucking wet." He brings his glistening fingers to his mouth and licks my juices off the tips of his fingers. He closes his eyes and lets out a low moan as he tastes me on his hands. "Fucking delicious, beauty. So damn sweet."

I know he is waiting for an answer, but I can't seem to find the words he was waiting for. All I can focus on are his fingers that are now playing with my clit, teasing their way along my seam.

He kisses me deeply, hungrily. I can feel his rock hard cock digging into me. I moan loudly, feeling anticipation building.

"Calum," I whisper, my hands gripping his shoulders. "Please. Don't make me wait anymore."

"Fuck, Kaia. Breathe, beauty…" His voice is husky, low.

I follow his advice, taking a deep breath to clear my ridiculously, pathetically aroused mind enough to whimper, "Please!"

He kisses the corner of my mouth and then starts to move down my body. Burning hot kisses land on my collarbone, my breasts, my sternum. He licks a ring around my belly button and I writhe against his body.

I can feel my clit aching, feel how fucking good his mouth is going to be when it finally touches my pussy.

I want him *bad*.

Calum kisses his way down my lower belly, to my thighs, around my sensitive mons. With his fingers he spreads my pussy lips wide.

"God damn, Kaia," he says quietly. He lays one kiss just above my lips. "Do you know how long I've waited to taste you?"

Without waiting for a response, he buries his whole face in my pussy, gorging himself on my taste, getting my scent and juices all over his mouth. Then he pulls back, licking slowly but hungrily along my seam. He lets out a low moan again. "So fucking sweet, Kaia."

He sticks out his tongue and swirls it around my clit, the part of my body that begs for attention. He groans and takes my sensitive clit in his mouth, sucking lightly, his tongue flicking against my bud.

I moan and touch my tits, grabbing them and pinching my nipples. The sensation makes my hips buck and my back bow.

His tongue quickly reduces me to a shivering, moaning maniac. I writhe my hips against his tongue, unable to contain myself any longer, but his strong hands on my hips hold me in place. He licks and sucks until I see nothing but stars and fireworks, feeling like I am about to fly away if it wasn't for him anchoring me.

The pressure that has been building up inside me releases into a bright ball of light. My mind shatters, shards falling every different direction. I scream his name, digging my fingers into his shoulders and tugging at his hair.

He keeps licking, swirling his tongue. I become too

sensitive and push at his shoulders. He looks up at me with the filthiest grin.

"You taste better than I could've imagined, beauty."

He raises himself up, coming up to kiss my lips hard. I can taste myself on his lips, earthy and salty and satisfying. There is something dirty and so intimate about enjoying his kiss just after he ate me out… and I can't get enough of it. I moan into his mouth and hear a low sound coming from the back of his throat.

"Don't stop," I whisper against his lips. "You promised to pop my cherry tonight. I want you to be my first, Calum. The only man I've ever been with."

His sapphire blue eyes snap open and he shudders. "Lay back, beauty."

He pushes himself to his knees and reaches over to grab one of the condoms. He tears the package open with his teeth, discards the package, and rolls the condom along his cock.

I bite my lip and watch. "I'm on birth control…"

Calum squints at me, smirking. "You don't have any way to know this, but that conversation is usually a whole different step. We can talk about that later, beauty. Right now, I just want you to enjoy yourself."

He pushes me back on the bed, settling himself between takes his cock and presses the blunt tip against the inside of my thigh. I pull him in with my legs, making him readjust a little until he settles the tip of his length against my wet pussy. We both groan in unison as he pushes inside, stretching me out with each inch.

I grip his shoulders, my nails digging into his flesh. His brow furrows in concentration as he works his length all the way in. My pussy clenches as I stretch and accommodate his massive size.

It hurts, honestly. Being so intimately stretched pinches painfully and having so the bulk of his weight on top of me is crushing me. He shifts his weight, taking it off me, looking down into my eyes.

"God *damn*," he murmurs. "Your pussy feels hot and wet and tight all at the same time, Kaia."

The reverent look on his face excites me. I provide something that he wants, which is new and exhilarating for me.

I move my hips, grinding my pussy against him. It rubs his cock against my inner walls in a new way, eliciting a ripple of pleasure.

"Fuck," I say, wanting more. "Please, Calum."

He looks up at me, a sheen of sweat beginning to break across his forehead. He moves then, slowly pumping his cock in and out of me. I start to feel ripples of pleasure, tentative at first, then more and more certain.

Calum takes my small breast in one broad hand, pinching the nipple. I start to move in time with him, rolling my hips. Little licks of flame start to unfurl themselves deep inside of me, stealing my breath away.

"God," I moan. Tossing my head back, I meet his cautious thrusts. He's being careful with me, but I don't want that. I toss my head back. "Fuck me like you own me. Fuck me like I'm yours and yours alone."

He stiffens for just a moment, then grabs my hips and pulls me up a few inches. He forgets his hesitant rhythm and starts hammering himself in and out of my pussy. My eyes widen for a second. He starts sweating in earnest, his sweat mixing with my own every single place that my fingers touch.

Looking at his fierce expression, I'm unsure what I've unleashed in him, more beast than man. But at the same time, the ripples of my inner pond are growing in size, becoming chaotic.

It feels unbelievably good to move my hips in time with each thrust. I'm compelled to match his pace, to meet his hips, to wrap my legs around him and draw him in more. I focus on that, letting my eyes drift closed, my fingers reaching for my own nipple. Calum groans, slowing for a second. He raises himself up and starts thrusting again. Then he pushes my hand aside, slipping his hand down between us.

He brushes my clit and my back bows. I feel like my hips are growing heavy and full, each of his thrusts bringing me closer to the edge of an abyss.

This is why people fuck. This sensation, this exact feeling I'm feeling right now. I understand completely now, where before I felt slightly out of the loop.

"Tell me what you're feeling," he mutters. "Talk dirty to me, beauty."

I look at him, at his beautiful chest, every muscle gleaming and straining. I don't know where the words come from, exactly, but as soon as he asks me, they burst forth.

"I love how your cock fills my pussy," I say, working my hips. "I love the way your fingers feel on my clit, baby."

He growls and redoubles his pace, hammering himself into me, his fingers working quickly circles over my clit. I suddenly feel electrified, moaning and clutching at his shoulders. He punctuates each thrust by stroking my clit.

"Come for me," he whispers, his words a plea and a command at once.

I clench my eyes shut, stretching, reaching for some unknown goal. "Calum… I…"

I reach a sudden cliff, running up one side and launching myself off. That's what coming feels like — falling down a deep, dark crevasse, seizing up, my whole body shaking and clamping down. Feeling a million tiny jolts of sensation overwhelming my entire system, all at once.

I open my eyes and keep my hips moving, trying desperately to breathe. He hammers his cock home at a blistering pace, his movements freezes as he approaches his own peak.

"God damn," he whispers, pumping his hips madly. "Fuck, Kaia, you're making me come…"

Then he roars, thrusting hard and raggedly a half dozen times. I feel him coming, feel his semen fill me in hot pulses. I can only turn my lips up to his once more.

In the moments that we lie here, struggling for each breath, I turn to him.

"Thank you," I whisper.

Calum turns his head to regard me. "For what?"

My cheeks color. "For making my first time memorable."

"Hm." He looks up at the ceiling. "I just didn't want you to regret it, beauty."

I study him in profile; look at him now is like admiring

a piece of art. I reach out with trembling fingers, touching his cheek, tracing his jawline.

"Did you regret it?"

He exhales and looks at me. There is pain in his eyes, honesty and torment.

"No. But what do I know? I'm fucked up. I'm broken."

I raise my eyebrows. "What? You're not broken."

Calum turn his head and pins me with his ocean blue gaze. "Kaia, if you think that I'm fine, you haven't been listening. I'm damaged so irreparably, gone past the point of return. Why else do you think I pay you?"

I start to answer his question, indignant. Why would he say such mean things about himself?

Then I pause. This needs an especially light touch.

I suck in a breath.

"I don't know what you've been through, Calum." Finding his hand, I twine my fingers with his, gripping hard. "But I will say that I collect broken things. Things that no one else wants to save, things that other people think are garbage. They have a home with me."

He squeezes his eyes closed for a long moment. The sound of his deep breaths fills the space between us. Then he looks at me, his hand coming up to cup my jaw.

He doesn't say anything. He just kisses me hard, his lips almost brutal as they find mine.

When he's done, he pulls me close. And I cuddle against him, wondering sleepily what makes a man like Calum tick.

CALUM

I sit in my home office, staring out the huge window into the Manhattan skyline. Behind me on my desk there is a stack of legal papers that I need to review. Things are beginning to slip through the cracks, what with me tied up at the ballet… and with Kaia getting under my skin at night.

But I don't look at any of the time-sensitive papers. No, instead I stare out the window and think about last night.

Skin on skin.

Our breath mingling.

Our naked, sweating bodies writhing.

She set my fucking soul on fire.

But Kaia still got up this morning and went to the New York Ballet, saying she had a costume fitting to finish.

I didn't want to let her leave my sight… but I can't just keep her trapped here.

…could I?

I cock my head, trying to imagine how I might be able

to get away with it. After all, almost anything is achievable with enough money…

"Calum!"

I spin in my chair, hearing my brother's voice. Arching a brow, I call out to him.

"In here, Lucas!"

A few second later, he appears in the doorway, looking testy. "Did you see our stock prices this morning?"

I suck in a breath, leaning back in my chair. "No."

He gives me an odd look. "Well, we have to figure out a backup deal since you punched Jack Schwartz in the face, Calum. There are starting to be whispers that we didn't have a second choice lined up."

I squint at him as he comes in, plunking himself down in a leather chair. I school my expression.

"Well, we didn't," I say at last.

Lucas tilts his head to the side. "Okay, what is going on with you? Normally that kind of news would have you screaming and pounding your fist on your desk."

I steeple my fingers and stretch my neck. "I'm not sure what you want from me."

His gaze scans my face and my body language. For a long moment, he's silent. Then he leans forward, a smile playing about his lips.

"You got laid," he says. He purses his lips. "I'm right, aren't I? You got your dick wet and you forgot all about your real life."

I shoot him a glare. "Fuck off."

"Ah!" He claps his hands a few times, reclining in his seat. "It must have been good if you're being secretive about it. Tell me, was it someone taboo? Maybe the daughter of a competitor?"

I stand up, giving him a look. "We should change the subject."

Needing a cup of coffee, I head out of my office and down the hall toward the kitchen. Lucas is right on my heels and he's not done guessing.

"Wait, I forgot. You haven't been at work. You've spent all your free time training ballerinas." He goes silent for a moment. "Oh, Calum. Please tell me it's not one of the girls from your ballet."

I walk into the kitchen and flick on my coffee grinder. It whirs to life, loud enough that it makes conversation impossible. As soon as it stops making noise, it starts brewing the grounds into a fresh pot of coffee.

When I turn around, Lucas is leaning against the kitchen island, a grin on his face. "Who is it? Did you finally woo Honor into fucking you?"

He raises his hand, rubbing his fingertips together to signal money. My neck heat and my hands clench into fists.

He's not wrong about my method. I do like to snag girls with money. It's just easier to pay them and know that our relationship is transactional. He just isn't up to date about the whole Honor situation.

"Is there something that you want from me? Or can I get back to going about my business?"

He rolls his eyes. "You are no fun. I just came to say that I was at a board meeting this morning and your personal stock price is dropping like a fucking stone."

I shoot him a glare. "If I make you acting CEO, will that embolden you to get the fuck out of my kitchen?"

The smile drops away from his expression. "Seriously?"

"If the company needs it? Yes. I've been on autopilot mode for weeks. Might as well make you the CEO…" I pin him in place with a glare. "I swear to god, Lucas. If you fuck this up, I'll take it out of your hide."

His hand flutters in the air between us. "No need for threatening me. IndicaTech is as much my baby as it is yours."

I flap a dismissive hand at him. "Fine. I'll step down while my attentions are divided between Indica and the NYB."

He screws up his face. "Please tell me that you aren't just going to dump the whole Jack Schwartz problem in my lap."

I give him a thin smile. "No. I'll keep working on that."

"Good. I don't know any other kind of blockchain technology that exists that is as powerful as Schwartz's."

I narrow my eyes at him. "If it were easy, I would have done it by now."

He licks his lips, about to fire back his response. But luckily at that moment, a loud chime begins to sound.

I turn my head toward the panel on the wall, which is currently lit up. Walking over to it, it press the intercom button.

"Yes?"

A video screen turns on, Honor's face smiling seductively to the camera. "It's me, Cal. Let me up."

Her shortening of my name — calling me Cal — sends an ugly shudder down my spine. The only person that has ever called me that is Anita.

"So it is Honor," I hear my brother mutter behind me.

I glare back at him. "I told you, I'm not sleeping with her."

I do need to talk to her, though. Pressing the intercom button again, I say, "Come up."

I turn to find Lucas heading out.

"Wait," I call to him. "I don't want to be here alone with her. Honor has already filed three lawsuits against NYB for ageism and sexual harassment. It would be better if there was a witness here."

Lucas turns to me, his eyebrows rising. "Uh… sure," he says with a shrug. He squints. "It's really not her, then."

Shaking my head, I pour myself a cup of coffee. Lucas fixes himself one too.

Then we stand, sipping the steaming brew, and wait.

It doesn't take long before the elevator chimes. I lean over and press a button, allowing the elevator doors to open. The sound of heels clicking on stone grows closer and closer.

I look at Lucas, nodding toward the living room. He follows me in, still sipping his coffee, his expression perfectly blank.

I swing open the front door. Honor gives me a sultry grin, her blonde hair falling in waves over the top of her black trench coat.

"Hey Cal," she says playfully. She wrinkles her nose, stepping closer. Her lips are slicked with bright red gloss. "Are you going to invite me in?"

I squint. "Do I have a choice?"

She titters at that, reaching out a slender hand to push me back. Not interested in having any kind of contact with her, I step back before she touches me, turning and heading into the living room.

Honor follows, pulling up short when she sees Lucas. "Cal, you didn't say that there was anyone else here."

I clear my throat and sink into an armchair. "You can address me as Calum. And you didn't ask if I was alone, Honor. Just like you didn't ask if you could come to my private residence."

Lucas sips his coffee stoically, giving her nothing when she looks to him for help. She glares at him.

"It would be better if we talked alone."

I glance at my watch. "No. Do you want to go first? Or should we just speed things along here?"

She narrows her gaze on both of us. "I think we got started on the wrong foot, Cal—"

"Now it's Mr. Fordham," I say. I cross my arms and cock my head. "And you have two minutes to get to your point."

"Well," she says, smiling broadly. She glances at Lucas and then back to me. "I had hoped for this to be a matter between us. But since you don't care, then I suppose I won't either." She pins me with a huge smile. "Marry me, Calum Fordham."

I give her an incredulous look. "I'm sorry?"

She walks over to where I am sitting, touching my hand lightly. "You heard me. You've wanted me for years. Now here I am. Asking you to make me Mrs. Fordham."

I gaze up at her, not quite understanding. "What on earth are you talking about?"

She looks over at Lucas, crinkling her nose as if I'd just made a joke. "Is he always so hard of hearing?"

I start to rise. "Listen up. I talked to Kaia. She told me about what you said to her. And I just want to make something crystal clear." I pause, leaning forward. "There is never going to be anything between us, Honor. Not to mention the fact that I already know that you're fucking pregnant with Mikhail's child."

Honor smirks a little, rubbing her hand over her stomach. "It doesn't have to be his. It will be yours, if you marry me and put your name on the birth certificate." She wrinkles her nose. "Just like that, an instant family. Plus you'll get me, any and every way you want me." Her lips quirk. "Don't pretend like you didn't masturbate to me a couple of hundred times over the years. Don't act like I'm not offering you something you've coveted forever."

My eyes tighten on her face. Several seconds tick by and a smile plays over my lips. "I'll pass. We should talk about what will happen to you and your unborn child if you ever threaten Kaia again, though. I promise you, it won't be pretty."

I glance at Lucas and he scowls at me.

"What?" I snap.

"Who the fuck is Kaia?!" he whispers.

I flap a dismissive hand at him. "Doesn't matter."

Honor crosses her arms, sneering. "What, you don't want your brother to know about your dirty little secret? Cal is fucking one of the little girls he hired to replace me at the ballet. Judging by the photos my private investigator got of you two canoodling all over the fucking city, you have a type. Young, blonde, and flexible."

Her lips twitch. I blink, trying to rein in the immediate fury I feel.

Lucas climbs to his feet, scowling at Honor. "I think you should leave."

She rolls her eyes. "Yeah, right. Here is the deal, since you had to make me play hardball. I want three hundred million dollars as a fee for keeping those pictures to myself. I want your stupid little bimbo fired from the company. And I want you to sign your name on my baby's birth certificate, so I always know that he'll be taken care of financially."

I scoff. "Just because you have some fucking pictures?"

She smirks at me. "I have a video from inside Club X, okay? You and your newest little blonde, in the champagne room, talking about your filthiest fantasies. And the second I turn them over to the press, they will tear her to pieces. Your reputation may be tarnished, but she'll be ruined. She won't dance anywhere ever again, ballet or otherwise."

I glare at her, but inside I get a sinking feeling in the pit of my stomach.

I know what the ballet means to Kaia. I know how hard it would be for her to lose her position in the company… and be hounded by the press.

Deciding to bluff a little, I stand up and cross my arms. "I don't think that this alleged video will do the damage that you think it will. And I don't really care for Kaia, so…"

She smirks at me. "Yes you do. I saw you two together

at the bar. When you thought no one was looking, you acted just like a man in love. Whatever you may say, I know that you're weak where it comes to women."

I scowl at her. "You don't know me."

She tips her head to the side. "Yes I do, Cal. I've known you and men just like you for my entire life. And in order to get what I want, all I have to do is endanger the princess in the castle. You'll get your knight's armor on and ride out to save her. You can't help yourself." Her lips quirk. "It's pathetic."

My fingers flex, aching with the need to wring her neck.

"Oh, I almost forgot." Honor smiles at us both. "If I don't get my way, I have already paid for a contract with the Ukrainian mob. Unless I'm made very, very rich and very happy, it goes into effect."

She withdraws a piece of paper that has been stamped with a photo and vital information.

Kaia stares back at me, her doe eyes wide, her lips parted as if she's about to speak.

I look up at Honor. "You're…" I chuckle, not knowing how else to respond. "Fucking insane."

She bites her lip, smiling, and shrugs. "There are worse things to be, darling."

"You're going to end up dead," I tell her.

She starts backing away slowly. "I will give you the night to break the news to your little fuck doll. Tomorrow morning, I'll be back with the papers for you to sign. You should…" She waves her hand. "Call somebody that can arrange a large transfer of funds."

Glancing at Lucas, I don't even know what to say. "You're literally nuts, Honor."

She winks at me. "Test me, Cal. Find out just how fucking crazy I am."

Then she whirls and struts away, her heels clicking on the stone floors as she goes.

I stare after her for a long moment. Lucas clears his throat.

"Is she right?" he asks.

I look up at him, overwhelmed. "What?"

"Do you… have feelings for this girl? Because if you don't, then Honor has basically nothing on you. You can just walk away."

Shaking my head, I drop my eyes to the picture of Kaia again. "I don't love her. I'm not even capable of that."

He sighs. "No one is throwing around that word but you, Calum. I just asked if you care about whether she gets hurt or not."

A tendril of emotion creeps out as I stare at her picture. "Maybe."

"Well… then things are about to get difficult," he says.

Bile burns the back of my throat. "I know."

I drop the photo to the floor, turning toward my office. Lucas squints and follows me, not saying a word.

KAIA

*C*alum is late.

I shiver as I glance at my phone again. I'm waiting for him outside of the Continental, the hip, sleek bar at the bottom of his building. He asked me to meet him here twenty minutes ago… but so far, he's a no-show.

And I'm way too much of a wuss to try to go inside with Calum there, paying the door guy off.

Are you close? I start typing into my phone.

A hand lands on my arm. I startle and look up, flush at the sight of him. He looks a little disheveled, his hair raked to the side, his tie loosened. He's still wearing his suit but his suit seems rumpled. His eyes lock in on me, expression unreadable.

He jerks his head toward the bar. "Let's go."

I frown as he ushers me into the bar. His apartment is only an elevator ride away… but I guess he just wants a drink. I slide my coat off and he leads me to the bar.

Calum pulls out my chair and I sit down, my cheeks

flushing. I expected some sort of compliment on my dress, maybe a dirty thought whispered into my ear.

But I guess not. He seems preoccupied, busy thinking about whatever it is that billionaires think about, I guess.

I nod uneasily. He waves his hand at the bartender, who scurries over.

"What can I get you?

Calum looks at me, raising his brows expectantly.

My cheeks warm. I straighten my spine and clear my throat. "Yes. Could I have a French 75?"

Calum looks at me, his tongue darting out to wet his bottom lip. "I'll have a McCallum, neat."

The bartender nods and head off to start making the drinks. I turn toward Calum, reaching out to touch his knee.

"I expected to see you earlier today," I say gently. "We had out first rehearsal on the main stage—"

"Kaia," he interrupts, frowning. "I just had a talk with the ballet company. We are letting you go."

I freeze. My heart beats painfully in my chest. "What?"

His head bobs. "Sadly, I think that brings our professional relationship to a close."

"I'm— I'm fired??" I say, struggling to understand.

Calum reaches into his suit jacket, withdrawing a slim envelope and placing it on the bar before me. "I also wanted to let you know that your services will no longer be needed for me. I've paid you the entire amount that our contract stipulates--"

I grab his arm, forcing him to look up at me. "What is happening?"

The bartender comes back and drops off our drinks. Calum's gaze slides to him before settling back on me.

"I need to sever any relations we have, completely and finally. Do you understand?"

I'm so floored that it takes me a few seconds to answer that. "No, I don't *understand*."

My voice rises. He looks around, drawing my attention to the other patrons in the bar.

"Control yourself. We are in public," he says.

"Why are you doing this?" I ask. "Is it… is it because we had sex?"

Calum's face twitches. "No. It's got nothing to do with you."

"It sure as hell seems like it has everything to do with me," I say, bewildered.

He clears his throat, standing up. He taps the envelope between us. "You will find that I compensated you more than adequately. My suggestion would be that to take this money, find a ballet in another city, and start your life over again."

I don't know why, but suddenly I'm so angry at Calum. He can't just do this to me. He may be rich but he's still a person, ruled by the same things as me.

In a flash, I yank my French 75 off the bar and toss the contents in his face.

He blinks several times, startled, and wipes away the sticky sweet mixture that is trickling down his face.

"Kaia—"

"No!" I shout. I get off my stool, grabbing my coat. "No way. You don't just get to walk all over me. I'll… I'll sue the hell out of you and the NYB."

His hands flex into fists. "No you won't. I'm paying you enough money to silently fade into the background."

I pick up the envelope, my hands shaking, my eyes filling with tears. Then I look him right in the eye and start tearing it apart. "I'm not interested in your money, Calum. I want to be treated like a human being."

We stare at each other for several seconds. My face crumples.

He is a fucking bastard. Then again, he told me that the first time we met.

When someone tells me that they are broken, that they are a bastard, that their alliances aren't to anything but money…

The next time, I'll believe them.

Spinning on my heel, I race out of the bar, tears staining my cheeks.

$\mathcal{C}$alum and Kaia's story isn't over yet, not by a long shot. Raw, gripping, steamy, and emotional... Get ready for more of their story by grabbing The Dancer right now.

Want a little more of their love story? Get a deleted love scene right now by joining Vivian's mailing list.

ABOUT VIVIAN WOOD

Vivian likes to write about troubled, deeply flawed alpha males and the fiery, kick-ass women who bring them to their knees.

Vivian's lasting motto in romance is a quote from a favorite song: "Soulmates never die."

Be sure to follow Vivian through her Instagram or join her email list to keep up with all the awesome giveaways, author videos, ARC opportunities, and more!

VIVIAN'S WORKS

RUINED CASTLE SERIES
Forbidden Billionaire Romance
THE SINNER

The Beast
The nanny
The caress

Broken Slipper series
Forbidden Billionaire Romance
The Patron
The Dancer
The Embrace
Possessive

Ravaged Dream Series - coming 2023
Forbidden Billionaire Romance
The Rogue
The Intern
The Secret

Married At Midnight Series - coming 2023
Forbidden Billionaire Romance
Deal With The Devil
Lie Like The Devil
Forever With The Devil

Dirty royals
Forbidden Royal Romance
The Royal Rebel
The Wicked Prince
His Forbidden Princess
Royal Fake Fiancé

Lyon Dynasty world

Dark Billionaire Romance
KING'S CAPTURE
QUEEN'S SACRIFICE

SINFULLY RICH SERIES
Steamy Billionaire Romance
SINFUL FLING
SINFUL ENEMY
SINFUL BOSS
SINFUL CHANCE
SINFULLY RICH

HIS AND HERS SERIES
HIS BEST FRIEND'S LITTLE SISTER
CLAIMING HER INNOCENCE
HIS TO KEEP
HIS VIRGIN

THE ADDICTION DUET
ADDICTION
OBSESSION

OTHER BOOKS
WILD HEARTS

For more information....
vivian-wood.com
info@vivian-wood.com